The Sword of the Prophet

a novel

by Phillip Oliver Otts

"There is no hero but Ali, and no sword except Zulfiqar."
The Prophet Muhammad

"If there be one principle more deeply rooted than any other in the mind of every American, it is that we should have nothing to do with conquest."
Thomas Jefferson

Phillip O. Otts

Chapter One: Deception Indicated

Langley, Virginia

Martin always enjoyed his polygraphs. The exams were relaxing, even peaceful, in a strange sort of way. Most of all, they were quiet. No phones ringing, no urgent meetings in cramped offices or rushed conversations in narrow corridors, no rivals to avoid or thundering personalities to tolerate. The polygraphers took their time and the tests moved at a glacial pace, with restful interludes between questions and plenty of time to daydream.

Martin never told anyone about his unusual affection for the lie detector; he kept that little secret to himself, with good reason: his colleagues would assume he'd lost his mind and his inquisitors would conclude he'd become a dangerous sociopath. Their suspicious minds were only at ease when the subjects of their ministrations were visibly intimidated.

Now, there was a question that had always mystified Martin; how was a person supposed to act, when willingly submitting himself to a polygraph? Wasn't there something fundamentally wrong and wonderfully ironic about wiring a professional liar to a detector of lies? If there was a more bizarre, unnatural condition, short of torture, he had yet to encounter it.

On this particular morning, Martin was dreaming of his childhood. His mind held a perfect image of the barbershop in his home town. His grandfather was sharing a story with the old men who hung around the shop, men who knew each other's secrets and didn't mind sharing them, for a laugh. A younger Martin sat perfectly still, with his eyes closed and his elbows resting comfortably on padded armrests, just as he sat during his polygraph exam. The gentle buzz of the clippers and the comforting rhythms of the barber's hands carried Martin into a dream-like trance, the same feeling he enjoyed when wired to the life detector. Until today.

The polygraph machine emitted a steady, scratching rhythm as it traced little black lines on a paper scroll, like a seismograph of the soul. When the machine stopped, a chill raced down Martin's spine and he was instantly alert.

"I'm showing deception on the question of unauthorized disclosure of classified information."

The silence was shattered by the thin, brittle voice of the female security officer as she hovered over her equipment. She looked like a graduate student, far too young to understand the meaning of deception. Defiant in the face of panic, an irresponsible corner of Martin's deeply convoluted mind laughed at the irony. He had taken more polygraphs than he could remember during his many years of service with the Central Intelligence Agency and had never stumbled.

His defenses weakened after days of heavy drinking, Martin's weathered face cracked a slight smile.

That was a mistake.

The security officer, a pale young woman who worked hard to look plain, peered out from under her impressive brow, a continuous black strip that thinned slightly above her nose, and stared directly at Martin. With her dark hair tied up out of sight, her face looked pinched and for a brief moment, she resembled a faded photograph of her dead grandmother, a hard-headed woman of Greek Cypriot origins.

As Martin looked up, the young woman's features sharpened into focus and he saw her pale lips and thin jaw clench with determination.

"It's time to get serious. I'm showing deception indicated on the unauthorized disclosure of classified information. Now, why don't you tell me what's on your mind."

The young polygrapher was better prepared than Martin realized, as she practiced a trade inherited from her father.

Martin opened his eyes and stared at the pale green walls that reminded him of a jail cell he'd inhabited briefly as a young man and remembered why he'd never stumbled before: he'd never had anything to hide.

John Martin McCrary, an aging legend of the Clandestine Service, knew he was in for a very long day. If he'd known what lay in store for him, he probably would have stayed in bed.

It began just before dawn, when Martin woke to the sound of a burglar in the alley behind his modest bachelor's apartment in an older Arlington neighborhood. When he went outside to investigate, with a large flashlight in hand, Martin found a pile of wet garbage but no burglar, at least not the one he was expecting. As he reached down to lift a rubbish bin, the beam of his flashlight illuminated a pair of hissing red eyes, sitting on a box of half-eaten pizza. Deeply impressed, Martin was sure Daniel Boone himself had never seen a larger raccoon.

Being a step slower than his childhood hero and having no Kentucky rifle at hand, Martin was defenseless when the monster emerged from his dining place and latched onto his left forearm. Martin tried to pull back, but the beast was as big as a basset hound, too heavy to lift by its teeth. After three hard blows from Martin's flashlight, the raccoon rolled on the ground and twitched a bit before recovering and running off down the alley.

An hour later, after stopping by a walk-in clinic on his way to work, Martin learned he would have to be treated for rabies. "Don't worry, the shots aren't as painful as they used to be," the thoughtful nurse confided, as she cleaned Martin's wound and replaced his makeshift bandage.

Martin was in a foul mood as he drove east on Dolly Madison Boulevard toward the CIA's Headquarters complex in Langley, Virginia. His first reaction, when he encountered a traffic accident, was to ignore the old man and his Buick, but that wouldn't do. A middle-aged Boy Scout at heart, Martin thought he might change his own luck, if he stopped to help.

After parking his car behind the disabled sedan, Martin pulled up the hood on his jacket and slogged through the rain. Just as he reached the old man's car, Martin heard a honk and the sound of skidding tires, and glanced up just in time to see a Cadillac Escalade, moving in slow motion, as it rear-ended his cherished BMW and pushed it into the the old man's Buick. The huge SUV wasn't moving very fast, thank God, so no one was seriously injured. Martin's ankle was in surprisingly good shape, after rolling over in the wet grass. His vintage BMW didn't fare as well and would never be the same.

Later that evening, as Martin walked home from dinner at the Lost Dog Cafe, followed by a couple of drinks at the Stray Cat, his mind was troubled by primitive thoughts and ancient superstitions. If cats had nine lives, how many lives did he have? What about Karma? Was there something he did in a previous life, to deserve a day like this? Were his many sins finally catching up with him? How could he make amends, before it was too late?

Martin continued to grapple with these timeless questions as he trudged up the stairs to his second story apartment and fished for his keys. He wasn't alarmed when he heard footsteps on the third story landing but was caught by surprise when a tough-looking gnome handed him a large envelope.

"You're served," the little bastard said, while skipping down the stairs to the entrance below. Moments later, Martin learned his life would be disrupted by something worse than rabies; his ex-wife wanted more spousal support, and she was willing to hire the best lawyers to get it.

When his head finally hit the pillow later that evening, after nursing a few beers and contemplating his future, Martin was sure his famous luck had finally run out.

Chapter Two: A Woman's World

Fatima Lavasani walked slowly through a remote corner of the Grand Bazaar in Tehran, comforted by the familiar sights and sounds, the pleasant aroma of fresh spices and the bark of the market men as they pushed their carts down the narrow aisles.

She knew what she had to do, but had decided and undecided a hundred times, torn by fear, ravaged by doubt but finally overwhelmed by a particular sense of duty.

Fatima was a beautiful woman in her late forties. Without bothering to look, Fatima knew she had miscalculated by wearing a veil. The men of the market noticed her more for her slim figure and graceful walk than her face, which would have marked her as a wife and mother, projecting her status and enveloping her in an aura of respectability. The veil only heightened the mystery of her age, making her more conscious of herself and less sure of her decision.

It wasn't easy for a woman like Fatima to move about Tehran unnoticed by one of her acquaintances from the university, but she knew there was a small internet cafe behind a dress shop on the edge of the Bazaar, where a woman could find a few precious moments of privacy. She had a message to send to an old friend, a man she had known when she was young and free on the streets of New Orleans, in America.

Fatima flinched as a rush of images collided with the reality of her life in Tehran and her thoughts drifted back to memories of her father. Aref Lavasani had been a visiting professor of political science at Tulane University in New Orleans in the late 1970's. He was widely respected for his fearless opposition to the Shah and well known for his belief that Persia could become a prosperous democracy in the heart of the Middle East. His heart would have been broken by the tragic loss of life a month before, when the government used brute force to crush the protests that followed a stolen election.

Fatima replayed one of their last conversations in her mind. Tears filled her eyes as she listened to her father, a man with no sons, sharing words of wisdom with his only daughter. More than anything, Professor Lavasani believed in personal responsibility, the need to act in response to his convictions. He asked Fatima to understand why he couldn't take the easy road, the path followed by so many of his friends and colleagues, prominent Persian artists and intellectuals who abandoned their homeland for a comfortable life in Europe or America. The memory strengthened Fatima's resolve and helped overcome her fear.

Fatima's vision took a moment to adjust as she rounded a corner and moved from shade to sunlight. Squinting, she noted the small dress shop made of cheap cinderblocks, indistinguishable from the other shops in the alley if not for a blue sign hanging over a simple door made of unfinished wood. Fatima paused for a moment and ran her hand along the door frame as she glanced down the alley, surprised and disappointed at her inability to control her racing heart. Finally, with a scowl and a deep breath, she opened the door.

Brushing off her clothing as she entered the shop, Fatima was greeted in a cheerful tone by a woman resting on a stool.

"Good morning, sister, I've never seen you before. How can I help you? Do you need a dress for a daughter? Perhaps for yourself? May I show you some fabric?"

"Yes," Fatima responded, "Silk, perhaps? I need a dress for a celebration at home, a private affair, something modern and cheerful, Parisian?"

"Do you have a photograph or a pattern?" the dressmaker asked. "My sister and I can make anything with a pattern, even a dress you would never wear outside the home, something suitable for a fashionable woman such as yourself."

Fatima hesitated briefly, took a deep breath and said:

"My friends tell me you also have some computers with access to the internet. I was hoping I could use one of your machines to find a dress my friends saw on a European website. Can you help?"

The dressmaker smiled and nodded in response. Some women visited her shop to buy clothing, others came to use one of her computers, a clever idea devised by her younger sister, a worldly woman. She assumed Fatima had a secret lover or a relative living in London or Los Angeles, a foreign connection she wanted to conceal from the authorities.

"Certainly. The fee for using the computer is 5 euro an hour. If you buy a dress, I'll take that off the price."

Nervously, Fatima followed the shop keeper down a narrow hallway to a small, windowless room with a curtain for a door.

"Please, make yourself comfortable. May I bring you some tea?"

9

"Yes," Fatima responded, "that would be kind."

Fatima prepared a short e-mail to her friend Mariam Khoury, a Lebanese Christian woman and naturalized American citizen who had visited her during two trips to Europe, during the difficult years after Fatima's son, Omid, died.

Fatima prayed Mariam would still be able to find Martin. She blushed when she remembered how her friend told her about a recent encounter at her restaurant in New Orleans. Martin was older, her friend had said, but still handsome, with the same piercing eyes and warm smile.

"Martin was pleased to see me and asked about you, Fatima. He said he was still working for the government but was planning to retire soon," her friend said, "and, can you believe it, he's been divorced for years!"

Was it possible Martin still thought of her, the way she thought of him? Fatima chastised herself for thinking like a schoolgirl and remembered why she had to get in touch with Martin; her husband, a merciless man and senior officer of the Iranian Revolutionary Guard, was involved in something unspeakable.

Chapter Three: My Enemy's Enemy

Boris Nikolayevich Mystikov stood on the buried ruins of an ancient mosque, on the edge of the decaying Botanical Gardens in Tashkent, Uzbekistan. Once the fourth-largest city in the USSR and the regional center for Soviet power in Central Asia, Tashkent was now the capitol of an independent state. The sad condition of the gardens, part of a complex in northern Tashkent mirroring the ironically named Exhibition of Economic Achievements in Moscow, caused Boris to fume with resentment at everything he and Russia had lost when the Soviet Union collapsed.

The veteran KGB officer thought about his father, a man who sacrificed his life for a nation that no longer existed. What would the old man think if he knew his granddaughter was working as a glorified prostitute for wealthy businessmen in Moscow? What if he could see his grandson, a soulless computer hack and sycophant for all things American, wasting his life away in St. Petersburg and dreaming of emigrating to New York? The anger and bitterness rose in his throat and emerged with a sharp growl. His vision darkened and he could feel the weakness in his chest where his heart heaved and thumped unreliably.

Boris ached for a bottle, to lose himself in a blizzard of vodka, but he wouldn't allow himself to be weak. For the first time since the collapse of the USSR, Boris knew exactly what he had to do.

The sun rose high in a clear sky as Boris nervously crested the top of a small hill, the dusty remains of an ancient mosque. A few minutes later, he saw the

11

bearded Iranian and moved quickly to intercept him near the decaying American gardens on the north side of the park. Boris selected the meeting site with a keen sense of irony; an acre or so of Central Asian desert had originally been cultivated to resemble the tropical American paradise of central Florida. Now derelict, the lost garden offered a dull image of the fate he had in mind for a certain icon of American frivolity.

Boris knew Ali would wait by a small foot bridge, exactly as he was told. Boris was fond of the younger man and always looked forward to their meetings. He was, after all, Russia's only penetration of the Iranian Revolutionary Guard. An agent with that kind of access was hard to come by.

"So, tell me, Ali," Boris began, as he approached his man at the agreed location. "Is it true your people once ruled this land?"

"Yes." Ali responded with a laugh, as he shook Boris' hand. "The Persians ruled all of Central Asia, long before the children of Russia were a gleam in the eye of some lost Viking."

The two men had an unspoken agreement. Boris accepted Ali's pride in the illustrious history of his native Persia, and Ali quietly accepted his subordination to a Russian master.

"Persians, Mongols, Russians; at least the former owners were neighbors, carving out a natural sphere of influence when they reached the height of their power. It's the Americans I can't stand, with their armies occupying two nations so close to our borders." Boris found it useful to remind Ali they were serving a greater cause;

it took the sting out of the cash-filled envelope he would pass at the end of the meeting.

"I think the Americans are eager to go home," Ali remarked. "I'm sure there's something we can do to encourage them."

"So it's agreed, then?" Boris asked.

"The decision was reached last week," Ali responded. "The generals are confident and our alibi is airtight. Who would believe the Shia and Sunni are capable of cooperation? It would be unthinkable, if it didn't make so much sense."

Boris and Ali had much to discuss as they strolled through the empty garden.

Chapter Four: A Gift from Allah

Usama Bin Laden sat alone in a small hut in the remote Pakistani province of Waziristan, near the mountainous border with Afghanistan. He wasn't feeling well and had avoided taking his medications because they made him feel nauseous. Tossing a large bottle of pills to one side, he leaned over to pour himself a cup of tea from an ancient iron kettle. With that simple task completed, he was ready to get back to work. He had to leave the village after sunset, but wanted to finish a new audio tape for his followers before he departed.

"Brothers," Osama began, while cupping a small microphone in both hands, "Allah, in his infinite wisdom, used the Great Satan, America, to remove the Lesser Satan, Saddam, so that you, his holy warriors, would be free to reestablish his true religion in Iraq, the first step in a great restoration. Who can doubt that Allah's hand was at work, as the armies of the infidel swept aside the deceiver Saddam and his followers, the non-believers? I know many of you lost heart some years ago, when the Americans and their allies appeared to defeat our Taliban brothers in Afghanistan. But take heart, that loss was a temporary obstacle, a test and a challenge for the mujahidin, to prepare us for the greater test to come."

Bin Laden took a sip of water and glanced at his notes before continuing:

"Who but Allah could have lured the Americans into such a trap, to invade an ancient and proud land so close to Mecca and Medina, to occupy Baghdad, the ancient capitol of the great Caliphate during the most glorious golden age of our religion? Who but Allah could have sparked the flame that will eventually lead to the unification of all Muslims against our common enemy? Who among you cannot see that the Crusaders are doomed to failure? The infidels were drawn like moths to the flame with dreams of stealing our oil, our riches and our dignity, only to be slaughtered by the thousands."

"Brothers, I had a dream not long ago. In that dream, I beheld the vision of a restored Caliphate, with its ruler sitting in a beautiful garden in Baghdad, on the day his armies recaptured the holy cities of Mecca, Medina and Jerusalem. In my dream, all this was made possible by Allah, as he rewarded the mujahidin for their perseverance and determination in their just struggle to liberate Iraq and the neighboring lands of the holy places from occupation and humiliation by the infidel."

"You, my brothers, are on the verge of achieving a great victory, which will lead to a great awakening of the Muslim community and the inevitable defeat and annihilation of our enemies. If there are any among you who doubt, strengthen your faith and behold as your enemy suffers, as you have suffered, and flees like a dog to lick his wounds, Insh'allah."

When he finished the recording, Bin Laden sat quietly by the open fire with his son, Awwab, who had recently traveled from the Pakistani province of Baluchistan to meet him in private. Bin Laden looked up with a patient smile but did not speak. He could see the eagerness in the younger man's eyes, so he nodded and signaled his willingness to listen.

"Father, I tell you the Persians believe I am a simpleton, a bearer of messages. They suspect nothing."

15

Bin Laden responded in the formal, traditional fashion dictated by his status:

"My son, no father could be more proud than I, for you have withstood the greatest test, living among the heretics in Iran, while strengthening your faith and advancing the great cause of Allah. The Persians think they are using us, but we will use them. Once we have obtained and used the weapons we need, the great Sword of Allah, we will reveal the source of the weapons to the Americans. I will send a message so you can leave Iran before that happens. Once the Americans have broken the backs of the Persians and we have turned the Russians and the Americans against one another again, we will launch our offensive and drive the occupiers from Iraq and Afghanistan in humiliation. Our victory will shine like a beacon everywhere."

Awwab responded with a deep sense of admiration:

"Father, I live for that day and only hope you will allow me to fight as you fought, with the holy warriors, so that I might truly earn your respect and bring honor to our name."

"God willing, my son, God willing," Bin Laden concluded.

Chapter Five: The Family Tree

Inman, South Carolina - 1954

A year or so before Martin McCrary was born, his father, Billy McCrary, stood at the base of the great obelisk built to honor the family patriarch and gazed up the granite shaft toward the heavens above. A few clouds raced by on a cold northern wind and that spun his head around. Drunk, as always, after losing at cards, Billy steadied himself with one hand and tried not to piss on his shoes. The warm water left his body with a sigh of relief and a puff of steam as he traced his initials on the cold stone, just below the old man's epitaph.

Fumbling with his zipper, Billy stumbled and fell flat on his ass, or, more accurately, Great Aunt Eudora's grave. Looking up, then down, Billy laughed at the image; his Grandfather's monument, the most famous phallus for miles around, stood stiff and tall, while his own penis lay weak and flaccid.

"Don't worry, little feller!" Billy said to himself, "You've been places that old bastard never dreamed of!"

"Get your skinny ass up off that cold ground, Billy McCrary! If your Daddy catches us here, it'll be worse for me than it will be for you!"

Bessy Jackson was the finest, fairest looking black girl for a hundred miles around. She was tall and thin as a willow, with long limbs, high cheekbones and coffee-colored skin, heavy on the cream.

Everybody knew Bessy's daddy was a white man, a handsome con artist who slipped in and out of town

17

during the Depression, on the slow train from Spartanburg. Some say that man took Bessy's momma without asking, and that's why she went crazy and never could love Bessy the way she should. But that didn't bother Bessy much because she could have as much love as she wanted, any time she wanted, from any man she wanted. And Billy was her favorite, her one-way ticket out of town.

"Come over here, Bessy, and sit down beside me. The car's all packed, but we're not going anywhere until you give me a kiss!" Billy was dangerously handsome, with a smile that could melt rock salt and blue eyes that never stopped laughing.

Bessy leaned against the '52 Buick, a black beauty Billy won in a card game the week before.

"You can forget about that, Billy McCrary, until you get me out of here, just like you promised!"

Bessy turned her back on Billy and crossed her arms across her chest, while glancing over her shoulder with as fierce a face her sweet, messed up soul could muster.

Billy staggered to his feet and stumbled over to the Buick, with his fly down and his shirt out. He grabbed Bessy by the hips and pulled her close. His hands pulled and tugged until Bessy's dress was gathered at her waist.

"Come on, girl!" he said, while touching her gently. "I know you want it just as much as I do."

Billy was right, Bessy wanted it, too, almost as much as she wanted to get the hell out of South Carolina.

"Oh, Billy boy, I bet you said the same thing to all those girls over in Korea."

"Shut up now, Bessy, I told you they didn't understand a word I said!"

Billy pushed Bessy down gently, until her forearms rested on the trunk of the Buick. He closed his eyes as he moved, with images of Asian brothels and broken soldiers flashing through his head, and came with a shout before resting his head on Bessy's warm back. The girl continued to rock her hips in a gentle rhythm, teasing Billy and making it clear she wasn't done yet. Billy laughed and reached down in response, only to stumble backwards as he was blinded by an unexpected light.

"You worthless piece of shit!" Billy's daddy shouted, as he knocked his son to the ground. Messing around with a black girl, in front of your Grand-Daddy's grave!"

Big John McCrary, the shotgun-toting Deputy Sheriff of Spartanburg County, was an angry man, red-faced and steaming hot, even on a cool night.

"Don't worry, Big Daddy!" Billy laughed, while resting on his skinny ass and his sharp elbows. "She's not the only one! I've left you at least two grandbabies to take care of, once I've left this shithole for good! Give it a few years, and you may recognize some of 'em!"

"What in the hell are you talking about!" Bessy shouted, as she stepped out from behind a tall camellia, still adjusting her dress. "Who else you been doing, you no-good bastard? Was it that bitch Tanya? I seen her smiling at you!"

Before Billy could answer, Big Daddy swung around and struck Bessy on the side of her head with his

19

right fist, a calloused hand that knew what it was doing. For a moment, Billy's feet wouldn't move as he stared at his father towering over Bessy's crumpled body. When Billy saw that hard, remorseless face, the same face that stood over his mother's casket all those years ago, he flew into a violent fury, worse than the bloodlust he felt when fighting for his life in Korea.

Before Billy knew what happened, he was standing over his father, with the business end of the old man's shotgun touching his barrel chest. Big Daddy didn't recognize Billy's twisted face at all, and he feared for his life. With good reason.

"Don't pull that trigger, son! You want to spend the rest of your life in prison? Don't worry, now, I'll clean up this mess and we can move on. We'll get you some help at that hospital down state, so you can put that damned war behind you!"

With a rush of adrenaline, Billy's head was clear. He stepped back, but only after removing the revolver from Big John's holster.

"No, Daddy, I won't shoot you. I do wonder what you're gonna say, though, when the Sheriff finds you laying there with whiskey on your breath and both your guns missing."

Having said all he had to say, Billy struck his father on the side of his head with the butt of that shotgun and knocked him senseless. Before walking away, he poured the remnants of a bottle of Jim Bean on the old man and dropped it by his side.

The young man hadn't cried since his Momma died, but he cried for the father he wished he'd had, but never would, at least for a few minutes. After that, Billy pulled himself together, just like he did when his best friend got himself killed in Korea, and put Bessy in his car. He figured she would land herself a fine job in Las Vegas. A beautiful girl like that, and a fine dancer, too; she could write her own ticket!

Billy had been around long enough to know the folks in Vegas weren't too picky when it came to shades of brown, as long as the person in question had tits, talent and a beautiful face. And with him winning at the tables, they would make one hell of a couple, that's for sure!

Billy had left his home town before, but this time was different. He never did come back.

Chapter Six: Holy Warriors

Sweating from a hangover, Martin sat on the back pew of the Great Awakening Church in Biloxi, Mississippi. He didn't want to offend his cousins, who had invited him to attend Sunday services during a brief visit, but he wasn't listening. He spent most of the sermon in a debate with himself, trying not to rehash all the regrets about the impending end of his career, while failing to persuade himself he would be better off retired. He was slowly driven out of his musings by the powerful voice of Reverend Robert Wilkins, the famous tele-evangelist and guest speaker at the church that Sunday.

"Brothers and Sisters, there is joy in my heart! I believe the day is fast approaching, as foretold in the Bible, when Christ will return to claim His kingdom. I know many of you are confused by that great and final word, the book of Revelation, where the fate of mankind is laid bare. Fear not, for the meaning is simple, for those who will listen."

"The true Christian prays with all his heart for the Second Coming, and who can doubt the time approaches? God's chosen people in the nation of Israel are surrounded by enemies. Our blessed land is engaged in a struggle with the army of Satan, the Muslim terrorists of the Antichrist who profess an evil religion and threaten to kill or convert us in the name of their false prophet, Muhammad. Our great nation is being lead by a socialist, a 'COS-MO-POL-I-TAN' man who believes in world government. As a result, our economy is in ruins and millions continue to lead sinful lives, when God shaped us for a higher purpose. Prepare yourselves and your families, with hope and joy in your hearts, so that we may be worthy of his Second Coming."

Martin was stunned and sat in silence as the Reverend continued to elaborate in a rich, silky baritone. A trickle of cold sweat ran down the back of his neck as he scanned the congregation. A few people seemed to squirm in their seats or stared nervously at their feet. Martin wondered what they were thinking. Did they disagree with the Reverend? Did his message threaten their comfortable lives? Or did they fear their sins would somehow drag them down at the moment of Rapture and leave them behind to suffer in agony?

Martin had lived abroad for most of his life. Every time he came home, he noticed changes in the country, and himself. Some of the changes were subtle, some more dramatic, and his reaction to the changes was often unpredictable.

Martin's response to the sermon was both physical and emotional. He felt a sharp pain in his gut and, for a moment, the aging spy feared he would puke on the floor beneath his feat. He turned inward, instead, with a feeling of hopelessness.

The rational portion of Martin's brain had long since given up on the notion that he could make any real difference in the world. The idealistic world view he cultivated as a young man began to crumble well before middle age and somewhere along the way he began to lose faith in God, in his country and himself.

The struggle began when Martin found he could no longer accept the usual explanations for the suffering of children, after seeing far too much of that in developing countries. The self-doubt grew when Martin saw how often his work destroyed the families of the men who spied for him. Far too often, the rewards were hardly worth the risk. Martin's sense of futility reached a peak when he realized he was a pawn in a game played by powerful men, cold-hearted bastards who heard what they wanted to hear and ignored the rest.

Early in his career, one of Martin's agents taught him a lesson he would never forget. The lesson was a reward of sorts, to recognize Martin's effort to put himself in the older man's shoes, to better understand and motivate him. The agent, a lapsed Catholic priest with ties to a violent communist insurrection in the Philippines, explained it this way:

"A man without hope or honor is content to pull the world down around himself, even to complete destruction. This truth is most evident when speaking of the young men who choose the gun or the bomb over a lifetime of backbreaking labor earning pennies a day so they can supply cheap goods to rich countries like yours. But Man is first and foremost a spiritual creature, in spite of his material needs and desires, and the day will come when even rich men will be content to pull the world down around themselves, for their hearts will be empty of joy and full of pain and their goods cannot fill the emptiness."

"This is true in my country, where the children of rich men serve as both our most heartless capitalists and our most ruthless terrorists - what irony, that these men should have so much in common. I believe it will someday be true in your country. Beware of men who pray for death and destruction in the service of their religion, for their prayers may one day be answered."

A lifetime of habits were hard to overcome. Martin was a man who had spent his career going out of his way to avoid attracting unwanted attention. He spoke quietly and usually revealed his passionate nature in private conversations.

Like many of his colleagues, Martin laughed at the popular image of the spy as super-hero: a handsome, athletic and supremely confident man who left a trail of broken hearts and lifeless corpses in his wake. Unfortunately, some of Martin's peers sought to breathe life into the stereotype and walked with more swagger than Dirty Harry. Others saw themselves as heirs to the British colonial tradition, proudly carrying the "white man's burden" in all of those brown-skinned countries that seemed incapable of governing themselves. Never mind the fact that Hurricane Katrina had exposed the truth, that America is much the same as any other country when its most precious asset, the rule of law, is torn away.

After years of experience in the field, Martin knew most foreigners despised overconfident, back-slapping Americans, even if they enjoyed watching Hollywood's action movies. The locals engaged in a kabuki dance they learned during centuries of domination by European colonial powers. They smiled and pretended to be impressed, but secretly dreamed of humiliating their new overlords, while exploiting their American contacts for personal, familial and tribal advantage whenever possible.

Martin wanted to stand up, but his backside was planted firmly on the pew and his feet refused to move. With great effort, Martin rose and inched past his cousin

Burt, who nodded his head as he listened intently to the Reverend.

Burt's wife, a pale, skinny woman who viewed Martin's foreign connections with suspicion, hissed at him as he passed:

"Marty, what are you doing? Sit down!"

Martin ignored the woman as he moved to the center of the aisle and looked directly at the Reverend. A handsome man blessed with more than a fair share of charm, Wilkins had a gift for engaging his congregations and was famous for his uncanny ability to make eye contact, to reach out with a quick smile that made people feel he was speaking directly to them.

The Reverend hesitated briefly, sizing up the situation and wondering if this average-sized but distinguished-looking man was overcome with passion and needed to declare his faith.

As it turns out, he was right, but for the wrong reasons. Martin hesitated before taking a few steps forward, so he could position himself in the middle of the congregation. A week before, Martin would never have done anything so rash, anything that might draw attention to himself. Now, everything was different. He shouted out loud:

"Don't listen to this idiot! Can't you see he's just as crazy as the Muslim fanatics he claims to despise?" Suddenly a stranger to himself, Martin felt as though he was watching his performance through the eyes of a bewildered congregation.

It didn't take long for the Reverend's "deacons," a pair of semi-professional bodyguards, to eject Martin from the sanctuary. Martin didn't resist, even when

Buddy Buxton, the meaner of the two deacons, roughed him up a bit. He welcomed the bumps and bruises, which dulled a deeper pain he couldn't heal.

Chapter Seven: Persian Fantasies

Iranian President Amahdinejad sat alone in his private study in Tehran, gathering his thoughts in prayer as he savored a sense of destiny and certainty. For reasons he didn't understand, Allah had chosen him to preserve the Islamic Revolution. Few knew how fragile the Revolution had become, even with the trouble the Americans were having with their wars and their weak economy. With help from the Grand Ayatollah and the Guardian Council, the Revolution had barely managed to survive the riots following the last election.

Ahmadinejad knew the Islamic Republic was surrounded by enemies, with powerful American forces occupying Iran's neighbors in Afghanistan and Iraq. Across the Persian Gulf, Iran faced the Sunni Arab puppet states, the decrepit Saudis and their lesser lap dogs, all of whom suppressed Iran's Shia brothers. The Revolution's internal enemies were no less dangerous; wealthy, educated Persians, many with relatives living in Europe or America, weak men and women dreaming of a comfortable life, with no cause they were willing to die for, no passion for their religion.

The truth came to Amadinajad in a waking dream; to ensure the survival of the Islamic Revolution, he only had to lure the Americans into attacking his country at a time of his choosing. The more forceful the attack, the better. A strike against his country's visible nuclear infrastructure would be best of all. Any of his people who died as a result would become blessed martyrs. He would welcome such a fate himself.

An American attack would rally the people, giving the leaders of the Revolution the power and authority to eliminate all opposition, forever. Even the most liberal Iranian intellectuals would embrace the regime and cry for American blood. After such an attack, no one, not the spineless Europeans, the calculating Russians or the so-called United Nations, would be able to stop his country from developing nuclear weapons. The Americans might delay that achievement, to be sure, but they wouldn't be able to stop it.

His vision was as clear as a sparkling fountain in the desert sun; who but Allah could have placed an inexperienced young man like Barack Obama in the White House? Did the President really believe Iran would allow America to complete the withdrawal of its forces from Iraq without suffering the clear and humiliating defeat it deserved? No, Allah would never forgive him if he failed to finish His work. And who but Allah could have used a fool like President Bush to remove Saddam, the man who had been the greatest obstacle to the rightful domination of the Persian Gulf by the Persian people? Indeed, who but Allah could have drawn Iran's greatest enemy into the perfect trap? Amadinajad knew only his faith and his willingness to seize this great moment in history would preserve the Islamic Republic, the protector of the oppressed Shia, the true believers and the loyal servants of Allah. The road would be long and hard; he expected no less, given the rewards of paradise.

On the distant horizon, his dream offered glimpses of the future that awaited the faithful: the Zionist state reduced to ashes, the Americans in retreat behind their distant borders, and the Islamic Republic preserved and triumphant. In his heart, Amadinajad believed this was the only road that could lead to the return of the Hidden Imam and the establishment of Allah's true religion in every land.

His vision and determination renewed by prayer, the President of Iran called for his special visitor.

Chapter Eight: Realpolitik

"Prime Minister, I have troubling news from Tehran."

Russian leader Vladimir Putin, still dressed in judo attire, wiped the sweat from his brow and tossed a fine Egyptian cotton towel into a wicker basket by the patio door.

"Walk with me," Putin commanded.

Most of Putin's personal aides were former KGB men, experienced operatives like himself with whom he had forged a bond of trust and a sense of mutual understanding. Leo Slatkin, a tall and intimidating man with a full head of salt and pepper hair, was no different.

"We've received a report from one of the best sources handled by our Residency in Tehran," Slatkin began. "It seems the Iranians are conspiring to place weapons of mass destruction into the hands of Usama Bin Laden and his followers."

Putin walked slowly down a smooth stone path leading to a grove of birch trees outside his suburban Moscow retreat. The grove was his sanctuary, in winter or summer. He was in no rush to speak, not because he was surprised, but because he hadn't expected the Iranians to move so quickly.

"I was under the impression the Iranians had no weapons of mass destruction to share, other than perhaps materials that could be used for a dirty bomb," Putin responded.

"Sir, the situation may be uglier than we suspected. The Iranians have located several sources of chemical and biological weapons, some inside the Russian Federation or near abroad. They are offering fantastic sums of money for materials and technology."

"That seems like a risky business, for the Persians," Putin remarked. "Do the Americans know of this?"

Leo shook his head. "Not yet, Prime Minister. Of course, the American intelligence services have asked for our assistance in collecting information on certain members of Al-Qaeda hiding in Iran. With your authorization, we've provided some tidbits, but the Americans don't know we have a source directly involved in the secret relationship between the Iranian Revolutionary Guard and Usama Bin Laden.

Putin stopped near the edge of the grove and his next move in the never-ending contest with the Americans was as clear and obvious as a game of chess with a child.

"Listen carefully to what I have to say, Leo. I am placing you personally in charge of this. You will direct the SVRR to restrict all reporting from this source to my office. Every man on the list must be cleared by me. We will continue to collect information on the Iranian plot and only when I give the word, not a day before, we will decide what we should tell the Americans. In addition, you will work directly with the FSB to uncover any plot to sell state secrets to the Iranians. Tell Yuri I expect a briefing in two days on this issue. You may go."

Leo nodded and returned quickly to the house.

Putin stood alone at the edge of the grove and stretched, a feeling of power rushing through his veins. Leo didn't know, of course, that Yuri Popov, the Director of the FSB, Russia's internal security service, was already involved in a secret program to ensure the Iranians succeeded in their conspiracy. Few knew how closely Russia's interests converged with those of the Iranians, at least for the time being.

Putin believed the most effective way to diffuse American power was to lure the Americans into overextending themselves, beyond the debacles in Iraq and Afghanistan and on to Iran and possibly even North Korea. Putin was determined to act before the U.S. economy could recover from its current recession because he knew the impact of a terrorist attack would be magnified many times over and the damage to American power would be deeper and longer lasting.

Putin laughed out loud at the irony, given the role the U.S. had played in Russia's humiliating defeat in Afghanistan. That debacle had contributed greatly to the downfall of the Soviet Union, whose destruction the former KGB man regarded as one of the greatest tragedies in Russian history. Likewise, in the years since 9/11, America had slipped from the pinnacle of its power and hegemony to the point where it had few true friends in the world. Putin was certain he had to act before President Obama had enough time to turn things around.

Like a martial artist grappling a much larger opponent, Putin planned to use the Americans' heft against them. He might never have the same opportunity again.

Not long after the Americans invaded Iraq, Putin decided it was in Russia's vital national interest to manipulate the Americans into an attack on Iran. An outright invasion would be better. To achieve this objective, Putin pretended to support the American goal of preventing Iran from obtaining nuclear weapons, using peaceful means. In fact, he had no intention of allowing the Americans to use diplomacy to achieve that objective, just as he had no intention of allowing the Americans to complete their withdrawal from Iraq without a humiliating defeat.

During the last years of the Bush administration, Putin had believed this approach alone would be sufficient to lure the impatient Americans into launching an attack on Iran. Unfortunately, President Bush became much more cautious at the end of his term. Putin was still amazed at the stupidity of a system that forced the Americans to change their leader every four to eight years. How inconvenient, when there was so much more the brash Texan could have done to undermine American power!

To provoke an American attack on Iran during the first years of the Obama Presidency, Putin had allowed certain figures in the Russian criminal underworld to profit from the sale of weapons of mass destruction to the Iranian Revolutionary Guard, under carefully controlled circumstances. Russian intelligence had learned the Iranians were planning to provide some of the weapons to Al-Qaeda, which had promised to use them against the Americans in Iraq and elsewhere.

The plot was an elegant one because no one in the West suspected there could be any serious cooperation between the Shia government of Iran and their Sunni enemies in Al-Qaeda, when in fact their short-term interests, and the interests of Russia, were in perfect alignment. All of them wanted to eliminate American power and influence in the Middle East.

When the time came, Putin would "warn" President Obama; he might even provide information that would allow the Americans to prevent an insignificant attack. In the end, a group of Chechen terrorists would be blamed for transporting deadly weapons through Iran to Usama Bin Laden. Who would suspect Russia of involvement in a plot perpetrated by their bitterest enemies, Muslim separatists from Chechnya, a tiny corner of the Russian Federation? Who would know a top Chechen terrorist was on Moscow's payroll and under Putin's control?

These means would lead to the end Putin desired: an American attack on Iran that might succeed, tactically, but was doomed to failure, from a strategic perspective. The Russian leader believed this attack, along with a hasty and humiliating final withdrawal from Iraq, would mark the beginning of the end of the American empire, just as the invasion of Afghanistan marked the beginning of the end for the Soviet Union. Only now, Russia would emerge stronger than ever, enriched by oil revenues that would quadruple following a major war in the Persian Gulf, with dozens of nations around the world looking to Moscow for leadership in containing the warmongering Americans.

Putin stood quietly at the edge of the birch grove and savored a rare moment of transcendent joy.

Chapter Nine: The Gambler

Las Vegas, Nevada - 1955

Billy McCrary sat in a heavy oak chair, with his arms tied behind him, a pillow case over his head and his bare feet jammed into the corner of a very dark room. He could hear muffled voices out in the hall and imagined they were deciding his fate. He was right about that.

"How did it come to this?" he asked himself out loud. Everything had worked out well at first. Sure, he arrived in Vegas with only $20 in his pocket, but he made over $80 at the blackjack tables his first night. That was more than enough to buy a hat and a new suit, with plenty left over for a cheap hotel room and a bottle of booze.

You see, Billy had a gift, or a curse, if you like; he never forgot anything he saw, even things he'd rather forget. He was also good with numbers, especially when it came to counting money. And, as he discovered during his first stint in prison, his manual dexterity was off the charts. Billy was proud to learn that, when he first met the prison psychologist to talk about his "rehabilitation."

"So, tell me, Doc." Billy asked. "What kind of job can I get with these magic hands?"

The bored, overweight prison psychologist looked up from his papers, with a Camel cigarette hanging out one corner of his mouth, and started at Billy for a moment before answering. Dr. Twittle had been around for quite a few years and didn't believe in rehabilitation, not one bit. He simply needed the job.

"I suppose you'd be pretty good at picking blueberries," Twittle said, before summoning the next inmate.

It didn't take long for Billy to get over his disappointment, for he quickly learned he had a gift for cards, any game of cards. He could deal faster than any man alive, and could remember every card he dealt. He was even better at remembering when he wasn't dealing. And that's how Billy McCrary made his first fortune, until he got caught.

Billy's musings were interrupted when the door opened. Two sets of large hands spun his chair around and ripped the pillowcase off his head. It was nine o'clock in the morning and Billy looked pretty rough, but not just because he needed a shave. He'd been knocked around by those same four hands, but couldn't resist a quick smile when he saw one of the boys had skinned his knuckles on Billy's unusually hard head. That was one of the first things Billy had learned in boot camp and the brothels of Korea; always hit a hard thing with something harder, and most heads were harder than a bare hand.

The two Italian boys stepped aside and the one with the bandaged knuckles tried to hide the evidence in his left armpit. A short, well-dressed man wearing wire-framed glasses and a crisp suit walked in with an air of authority.

"Well, Mr. McCrary, it's your lucky day!" the older man said. Billy was more than a little surprised to be greeted in such a polite fashion.

"Pleased to meet you, I'm sure," Billy responded. "I'd shake your hand, Sir, if I could." Billy nodded toward the back of the chair, where his swollen hands were still bound with cheap Manila rope.

"Tony, untie him," the older man ordered impatiently, as he pulled up a chair of his own.

As Billy rubbed his wrist, Mr. Valenti introduced himself and explained the situation.

"Here's the deal, McCrary. My partner in the casino business wanted you dead and buried last night, for taking money from us like you did." Mr. Valenti's partner was useful, when it came to the rough stuff, but he lacked subtlety. For himself, Valenti had learned he could make a lot more money if he took the time to spot useful talent, talent he could put to work in the right place at the right time.

Valenti looked over at Billy and continued:

"Lucky for you, an associate of mine has a special interest. It seems you got his daughter pregnant, and being a good Catholic, with a son who died in Korea when you were there, he asked my partner to let you live, if you'll agree to do the right thing."

"What the hell!" Billy thought to himself. His girlfriend, Maria Sedari, had promised she would keep that little situation to herself, until they could figure things out.

"I should have known Daddy's girl wouldn't be able to keep a secret!" Billy thought to himself.

"Well, please relay my heartfelt sense of gratitude to Mr. Sedari," Billy offered, stumbling as he tried to stand up.

"Sit down, sit down," Valenti insisted.   "You haven't heard the rest of the deal."   The trim Italian-American businessman leaned forward and relayed the full story, using the fingers on his left hand to check off every point on his short list.

"First, you're going to marry that young lady. To-night.   So clean yourself up and get ready.   Second, you're going to work at my new casino in Havana, start-ing next month. I could use a man like you at the black-jack tables, to keep an eye out for cheats, like yourself. My dealers tell me you're the best they've ever seen, so you should be able to catch the best and all the rest, right?   By the way, your wife will be singing in her fa-ther's restaurant, next door, until its time for her to lay up and have that baby.   If you behave yourself and prove your worth, you'll have a bright future, working on the right side of the deck, with a bonus every time you catch a cheat.   If you refuse our generous offer, my boys will take you for a long ride in the desert.   Understand?"

It didn't take Billy long to figure that one out:

"Mr. Valenti, I've been trying to get a job in a ca-sino ever since I got here, and Maria and I were plan-ning to get married as soon as we could, only I didn't have a steady job.   Please tell Mr. Sedari I'd be honored to be his son-in-law, if he'll have me."

"Well that's it, then," Valenti said as he stood up. "Tony, check Mr. McCrary into a suite on the 12th floor. Get him anything he needs, but make sure he shows up at the chapel at six this evening. Got it?"

"Yes, Mr. Valenti, six this evening."

Once Billy had a chance to clean up in the small bathroom in the hotel's "security" office, he walked a few steps behind Tony as they headed to the elevator.

"Good thing the boss told me not to mess up your face," Tony joked, as he glanced over his right shoulder. "It would be a shame to spend your wedding night with a a fat lip!"

"Yeah, Yeah," Billy thought to himself. "Your time will come!"

Chapter 10: A Voice from the Past

Many years after his father left Las Vegas for good, Martin sat alone in a hotel room in Biloxi, Mississippi, with a bottle of Bushmill's in one hand and a guide to the local casinos in another. He was on administrative leave, until problems with his polygraph were sorted out. Glancing at the clock, he shielded his eyes from the glare of the midday sun as it fought its way through a pair of paper-thin drapes and cheap plastic blinds.

Martin was tired and hadn't slept well for days. His rest was interrupted by dreams even the whiskey couldn't wash away. One moment, he was a small boy, locked in a closet in Beirut, punished for his refusal to speak French at the dinner table. He lay on his stomach in a pile of clothes, his backside bruised from repeated spankings. The next moment, Martin was a young man, running in panic, as explosions seemed to spring from each step, no matter which way he dodged. And then, the worst dream of all, because it was the closest to the truth; he found himself standing over his mother's grave, on a steep hill outside Beirut, feeling nothing, absolutely nothing, as he imagined her body rotting away, consumed by dark, swarming insects.

Martin had two choices: get up and get moving, or keep drinking in his room. Then again, he could get up, go out and drink. That sounded more interesting.

As he strode down the narrow hallway, Martin had to step around a service cart loaded with linens and toiletries. The cleaning lady was surprised but pleased when Martin greeted her in Spanish. Through force of habit, during a brief conversation, Martin learned where she was born (Matamoros, Mexico), how many children she had (three, two boys and a girl) and when she arrived in Biloxi (six months after the hurricane). She was naturally grateful when Martin gave her a tip, to buy something for the children she'd left behind with their grandmother in Mexico. Martin always found time to befriend even the lowliest service personnel: friendly eyes and ears to warn him.

His kindness was also driven by a deeper motivation, having spent the first few years of his life growing up in a hotel in pre-revolutionary Havana, looked after by a Cuban nanny. In the lost soul of his childhood, he still missed her more than he missed his own mother, the grasping daughter of a greedy Lebanese businessman. Ripped from the arms of his Cuban nanny when he was four years old, Martin was taken to live with his relatives in Beirut, until his father was released from a Federal penitentiary in Florida. By the time he left Lebanon, just before his 12th birthday, Martin had learned to speak French and Arabic, but he never felt truly at home, no matter where he went and no matter how well he appeared to blend in.

Martin moved quickly through the small lobby of his cheap hotel and hailed a cab to a glitzy waterfront complex. He worked his way through the ground floor to a second story restaurant and exited through a side door to a multi-story parking garage shared with the neighboring Heart of Dixie casino. Five minutes later Martin was sitting in front of an internet terminal offered as a free service for guests at the hotel. He paid no attention to the shabby young couple sitting in the corner as they scanned a website looking for creative inspiration before visiting a local tattoo parlor, and they paid no attention to the nondescript older man sitting behind them.

Martin loved hotmail and even owned stock in Yahoo. He felt it was only right, since he maintained no less than a dozen anonymous web mail accounts, like a drug dealer. Welcome to espionage in the information age.

In took no more than a few minutes to check for messages from one of his former agents in Tehran. Martin had terminated the relationship months before, without seeking authorization from his superiors, because he feared the Iranian would be captured and killed. Martin felt he had no other choice after his best Iranian agent was executed a year before, after one of his intelligence reports was leaked by a member of the Bush administration who wanted to justify a more aggressive policy toward Iran. When Martin returned from his last meeting with the surviving Iranian asset, he falsely reported the man had quit, of his own volition, because he feared for his life.

"No doubt that's why I flunked my last polygraph," Martin thought to himself, while typing away.

The inbox for the agent's anonymous web mail account was empty. On a lark, he decided to check one of his personal e-mail accounts on the same computer, a risky business he would come to regret. He tried to cover his tracks by leaving Yahoo, opening a new browser and visiting a few innocuous websites before returning to Yahoo. Martin scanned the list of subject lines, deleting unwanted messages as he went, but stopped when he came across a phrase that jogged his memory. The subject line for the e-mail read "A walk in Audubon Park."

43

"Dear Martin," the note began. "It's been so many years since we took our last walk together in New Orleans, before I returned to my country with my father. I've never forgotten that day and often think about what might have been, if I had stayed with you. I've grown older now, but I can still remember what it was like to be young at heart."

"My father, peace be upon him, passed away some years ago. Do you member how he always talked about the need for men and women to act in the face of evil? Although the Shah, the oppressor of his day, is long dead, it is in my father's memory that I reach out to you now."

"Martin, I need to pass an urgent message and a warning regarding a matter far beyond me. Having spoken to an old friend who lives in New Orleans, you must know where I am. If you can imagine the worst, another day that will become a cipher in the history books, you'll be close to the truth."

"I need to talk to you, as soon as possible. F."

Martin pushed himself back from the computer terminal and sat as still as a gravestone. A flood of memories rushed by, even as he struggled to make sense of what he'd just read.

Throughout his life, Martin suffered from an unusual affliction. He had a photographic memory, enhanced with the sounds, smells and vivid recall of the emotions he experienced.

As he grew older and his mind became crowded with memories, the gift that had served him so well in his unusual profession became more of a curse. For reasons he didn't understand, the recollection of past emo-

44

tional states became more intense and he suffered a form of vertigo as he shifted in and out of his most vivid memories. Over time, he learned to restrain the pain of remembrance, to maintain control over the present.

Or so he thought. Crystal clear images of his last moments with Fatima raced through his mind. They were walking in Audubon Park, in New Orleans, the day after a powerful thunderstorm. The grounds were covered with leaves and bits of debris from the live oaks that formed a majestic canopy over the damp sidewalk. Although Fall, it was a warm day, with wisps of steam rising in areas where the morning sun reached the ground.

They stopped and sat on a wooden bench, with no soul in sight. The bench was engraved with a memorial to a local bon vivant who passed away some months before.

Martin didn't argue with Fatima when she told him she had to return to Tehran with her father, now that the Shah was gone and there was hope for a future in Iran. He already knew her sense of duty and loyalty to her father were unshakable.

Fatima was young, not yet 20 years old. She was the only girl who ever captured his heart, who amazed him with the depth of her character and the power of her intellect. The truth was, he didn't feel worthy, didn't believe he deserved her, so that made it easier to accept her decision. Why would the daughter of a professor, the most beautiful freshman at Tulane University, risk her future with a poor boy on scholarship, the son of a convicted felon from South Carolina? Fatima's mother was dead and her father didn't have any other family to look after him.   What could he possibly do to change her mind?

Martin allowed himself to bask in the memory of Fatima's presence.   He could feel his arms wrapped around her slim frame as her head rested gently against his chest.   He had wanted her more than he'd wanted anything in his life but, for reasons he didn't understand at the time, the love he felt for her made him more respectful than he had ever been with any girl.

Martin had several casual lovers before he met Fatima and had always behaved as one might expect. But Fatima was different. The thought that she might see him as just another upperclassman trying to get laid filled him with self-loathing.   So, during the times they were completely alone and could have gone further, Martin and Fatima had never done anything more than kiss, embrace and talk softly for hours.

His right hand brushed against her long, black hair, which smelled of fresh rain and almonds.   She looked up and smiled a sad smile.   He lost himself in her eyes and heard her words as if she were whispering in his ear again:

"Martin, I won't forget you.   I'll write.   Iran is a free country now, so we can travel and see one another again.   My father will resume his position at the University in Tehran; perhaps I can accompany him when he travels abroad.   I'm sure he wouldn't mind if we stay in touch.   You'll see."

And then she was gone.

Chapter 11: Katrina's Wake

As Martin drove west along the Mississippi gulf coast toward New Orleans, his mind wandered back to another journey on the same coastal highway, after Hurricane Camille, more than 40 years before. He remembered his father, distracted and staring off into the distance, with a pained look on his rough, unshaven face, the face of a man who had been lucky to find work when he was released from prison. A younger Martin scanned the destruction on both sides of the highway with amazement. In his mind's eye, he could still see a massive ship laying on its side in the middle of the road, as helpless as a beached whale. The boy glanced briefly at his father, wanting to say something, but he knew he'd be better off if he kept his mouth shut.

Martin's reaction to the storm was confusing. He was thrilled by the excitement it brought to his otherwise mundane existence. He was terrified by the news he heard on the radio, that hundreds of people had died at that very location a few days before, and he was ashamed because he knew it was wrong to find pleasure in a disaster that caused so much suffering.

An older Martin smiled to himself as he returned to the present and remembered how often he had sought adventure, for adventure's sake, throughout his life. Years ago, he stopped asking why and simply accepted the fact that most people found secret joy in the wake of disaster, natural or manmade, unless of course the disaster affected them personally.

Martin's thoughts drifted back to a lecture presented by one his mentors at The Farm. A quiet but intense man in his early 60's, the veteran instructor stressed the need for his students to learn how to put themselves in their target's shoes, to manipulate and recruit them.

"The key to understanding your man," the veteran explained, "is to examine the gap between the life he lives and the life he would like to lead. If his reality falls short of his dreams, as it often does, find a way to bridge the gap. Understand his burdens, his duties and obligations, both real and perceived, and help him carry the load. Uncover his weaknesses, his foibles, vices and fantasies, and ask yourself how they might be exploited. Find out how he thinks and acts, when he's alone and no one's watching, and you'll have a better understanding of the real man behind the everyday mask."

The instructor searched the eyes of his audience before continuing in a quieter, more intimate tone. "You can start by thinking about your friends and relatives. I'm willing to bet all of you know someone who is deeply dissatisfied with his life, some poor soul whose reality falls well short of his dreams, someone incapable of carrying his burdens without assistance, someone with a vice he's trying to conceal or a fantasy he'd like to make real. My challenge to all of you is to use your imagination to figure out how you might offer a solution to that person's problems, if you had the considerable resources of the Clandestine Service to back you up."

Martin remembered the moment clearly, when he scanned the large lecture hall and observed many of his fellow students squirming nervously in their seats. No one wanted to believe someone close to them might be vulnerable to recruitment by a hostile intelligence officer, or that they themselves might be vulnerable. At that moment, Martin understood the huge advantage he held over his colleagues, most of whom grew up in privileged families and had never known hardship. To understand what a person might do to improve his lot in life, Martin only had to think of his father, or himself.

Years later, Martin understood more completely how his profession gave him a superficial understanding of other people, the same way a man who survived a disaster with his family intact could never feel the pain of a man who lost his. Martin's awakening took place when he spent a week hiding in Ethiopia, near the border with Somalia. A widowed mother of five cared for him in secret as he recovered from shrapnel wounds in his legs. She was the kindest person he had ever known, with her generosity rooted in the blood-soaked soil of experience.

That chapter in Martin's life began in 1998, when he recruited a Kenyan gun dealer to spy on a Muslim war lord in Somalia. Martin had some reservations about the case from the beginning, because he knew the Kenyan was cooperating with the CIA as a form of insurance, to protect himself from his rivals. Still, the pressure to collect information on members of Al-Qaeda hiding in Somalia was immense after the bombings of two U.S. embassies in east Africa, so Martin took a calculated risk.

The sites Martin selected for his monthly meetings with the Kenyan gun dealer were remote and the tradecraft he used had worked well for over a year. The Kenyan received a set of encoded GPS coordinates over the radio, the day before a scheduled meeting. When the Kenyan arrived by jeep at the proper location, in a remote stretch of open country near the Somali border with Ethiopia, he always found a brightly colored water bottle sitting on a rock. Inside the bottle was a cryptic note with another set of GPS coordinates directing the Kenyan to drive to a different location, an hour away, along a route that could be monitored by Martin and his security team from a safe distance.

Only this time, something went badly wrong. Martin still didn't know how or why it happened, but he could remember the sequence of events; he was watching the Kenyan's approach from a vantage point near the Somali border with Ethiopia, just before sunset. For a brief moment, he looked up and scanned the sky, his concentration broken by the drone of a propeller-driven aircraft. The sound was elusive, fading in and out on a stiff breeze, now becoming stronger and more certain.

Just as Martin was about to say something to his companions, a member of Martin's security team equipped with a powerful spotting scope shouted, "We've got company, at least three trucks, and they don't look friendly!"

No one had to say anything. All three of the Americans collected their gear and raced toward their lightly-armored SUV, which was parked behind a small knoll. Within seconds, the first mortar rounds struck and Martin stumbled. When he looked down, still dazed by the blast, he was shocked to see blood streaming from his right thigh and left ankle. The security team quickly hoisted Martin into the back of their SUV and ran for the Ethiopian border.

The last thing Martin remembered, before passing out, was the sound of another explosion that shredded the front half of the SUV, killing both of his security men. If he hadn't already been wounded himself, Martin wouldn't have been lying down in the back of the vehicle and he would have been killed, too.

Later, Martin learned how his Ethiopian rescuer found him lying by a deserted well, just outside her tiny village, the morning after the attack. The woman didn't know how Martin got there and Martin had no memory of fleeing the burned-out vehicle on foot. Martin's physical recovery was slow and painful, but the most difficult part came months later, when he met with the widow of one colleague and the parents of another. The two men saved his life, but he failed to save theirs.

After that, Martin was no longer a detached observer.

Martin was overcome by a terrible sadness as he drove west toward New Orleans. Sadness at the death and destruction in the city he loved and sadness at the ugly truth it revealed. At the same moment in history when American power reached its zenith and the pundits spoke triumphantly of the country's unrivaled power and glorious place in history, the thin veneer of pretense was torn away for all the world to see. Yes, America was rich and powerful, but the nation failed to take care of its own.

Martin's thinking was influenced by his unusual childhood in Havana and Beirut. He was an odd duck, to be sure, in the eyes of his schoolmates. More than once, Martin heard the parents of his American friends whispering about his foreign mother and his disreputable father, the convicted felon who brought shame and dishonor to his family.

As an adult, Martin was keenly aware his unusual career had changed him in unexpected ways. By learning to understand and appreciate the perspective of so many foreigners, he began to question his own assumptions about the world. Just as he lost his southern accent after living abroad for so long, he lost his ability to see the world through a purely American lens. This fundamental change in his thinking was brought to a head in the aftermath of Hurricane Katrina, when a vague notion that something was wrong grew into a burning conviction that his country was more fragile than he ever imagined. The shock came with the first televised images, when Martin recognized the death, the destruction and the abject misery on the streets of New Orleans. He had seen the same images in the slums of countless cities around the world, but never in America, nothing like that.

It was noon on a Tuesday when Martin arrived in the French Quarter, an island of prosperity surrounded by a decaying city. The scene reminded Martin of the impossibly grand capitols of Central Europe, cities that could only be understood from a historical perspective, as the former center of lost empires. Would the French Quarter survive, after losing so much of the surrounding city that sustained it? Or would New Orleans become an amusement park version of itself, with the city's working class replaced by illegal immigrants and foreign students on temporary work visas?

Martin parked his car in a hotel garage and walked out to the street. He looked around to get his bearings and took a deep breath, the better to appreciate the unique perfume of the city, a fragrant aroma of stale liquor, fried seafood and mildew. As he turned the corner, he spotted the Lebanese Taverna, with a newly painted sign hanging from a wrought iron balcony. It took a moment for Martin's eyes to adjust as he stepped into the dark restaurant and took a seat in a booth facing the door.

A waitress appeared and handed Martin a menu. A moment later, the owner of the restaurant appeared. She scanned the handful of patrons absentmindedly, as she had done so many times before, but stopped suddenly when she recognized Martin. She smiled broadly and Martin rose to greet her with an embrace and a kiss on the cheek.

"Martin, it's so good to see you!" Mariam Khoury said in French. "What brings you to our beautiful city?"

Mariam stood close to Martin and smiled broadly, with her hands on his forearms.

"I need your help, Mariam," he said quietly. "I need you to put me in touch with Fatima."

Mariam's smile disappeared and her face looked grim as she searched Martin's eyes.

"Come, Martin, let's have a chat in my office."

Martin followed Mariam behind the bar and up a narrow staircase to an upstairs apartment she used as an office and a refuge. Mariam owned several businesses in the city: the restaurant, a catering service, and a fine antique shop in the Garden District. She ushered Martin into the apartment, gestured for him to sit in an old mahogany chair by the window and filled her tea kettle as she dropped her massive key ring on a solid oak table.

"Martin, what in the earth is going on?" she asked.

"Well, Mariam, I received a note from Fatima. She seemed very unhappy and mentioned she was still in touch with you; I suppose you must have given her my e-mail address. I was hoping you could help me find a way to meet her."

"But Martin," Mariam objected, "that would be risky for Fatima. You may not know this, but I fear her husband is a dangerous man. The last time we saw one another, she wasn't herself. She was guarded and seemed miserable with her life in Iran, not only because her son had died."

As calmly as possible, while looking straight in her eyes, Martin explained:

"Mariam, I wouldn't ask if Fatima had not asked to see me herself. She said you might be able to help and I believe she's right. The only way Fatima can travel safely out of Iran would be to meet an old friend in Europe. You could invite her to join you for a shopping trip, as you've done in the past, and the rest would be easy."

Martin waited patiently as Mariam sat silently, her mind racing. She thought about her businesses and how she would manage a trip. She did have an invitation to attend a prestigious antiques auction in Vienna and she still had time to accept, if she acted immediately. A widow with grown children and competent employees, she realized she could choose to go.

And of course there was Fatima. She wondered if her husband was beating her again. She also thought of a very special friend who had expressed an interest in learning more about the Iranian. Although the thought caused her to flinch, she answered confidently:

"Martin, you're right, we have to help. Fatima would be welcome to move in with me, here in New Orleans, if she wants to leave Iran forever."

Martin leaned over and clasped her hands. "Thank you, Mariam, I knew I could rely on you, just as my mother said before she died."

Mariam lowered her eyes and nodded. "Yes, your mother was always kind to me, when others were not."

Mariam swallowed hard as she struggled to overcome feelings of guilt and shame, the inevitable offspring of the divided loyalties that plagued her life.

Although Martin sensed something was amiss, he ignored his nagging intuition and focused on the task at hand. "To protect Fatima, we mustn't tell anyone about our plans. Now, when can you travel?"

Martin listened carefully as Mariam explained.

Chapter 12: Siberian Sunset

Boris Nikolayevich Mystikov sat patiently as the crowd began to disembark from the Trans-Siberian express at the huge train station in Novosibirsk, Russia. Young soldiers on leave from long tours of duty in Chechnya, Abkazia or Eastern Moldova were greeted by their squat mothers in babushkas, heavy wool coats and felt boots. Tatar men with dark eyes glowing under fur hats hawked food from little stands on the platform. Tired-looking prostitutes with dyed blond hair stood near the taxi stand, hoping to catch a fare of their own from the men climbing off the train. Solid-looking policemen in dark wool uniforms cast sidelong glances at the girls, more interested in protecting their cut than enforcing the law. Beggar boys ran through the crowd, looking for a handout or a carelessly-placed bag to steal.

As Boris walked across the platform and through the station, one of the policemen nodded in deference, recognizing Boris as a man of influence by his bearing and his fine leather coat. A cold wind blew snow across Revolution Square as Boris walked toward his hotel, a seedy concrete high-rise with a faded, weather-beaten Hotel Siberia sign on the roof. Viktor Viktorovitch Yadnikov, a retired Russian army officer and expert on chemical and biological weapons, was waiting in the spacious but poorly-furnished lobby when Boris arrived.

As the two men embraced, Boris suggested, "Come Viktor, let's have a drink."

Boris selected a table against the wall in the hotel bar, near a frosted window with pale yellow paint peeling off the frame. He opened the "fortochka," a small window used for ventilation in stuffy, steam-heated buildings, and nodded with satisfaction when he confirmed the traffic noise would make their conversation more difficult to overhear.

"So, Viktor, how are things?" Boris asked.

"Fucked up, as always," Viktor responded. "As you know, my pension isn't worth a bucket of piss. I've been working for a Japanese company, making pesticides. The fucking Japanese act like they won the war, Siberia is crawling with them. And now the fucking Chinese, the little yellow bastards, are setting up shop, selling all of the cheap shit the Americans won't buy. I've fucking had it."

"Well, Viktor," Boris began, "it's a crying shame for a man who risked his life for our motherland, as you did, to end up working for the Japanese. I remember when you were a top researcher on the island, with 100 dedicated young men working for you and the honor and recognition you deserved."

Viktor nodded and looked down into his glass. He burned with anger when he recalled the day his unit was ordered to pack out before abandoning the Soviet Union's premier biological weapons facility on Resurrection Island in the Aral Sea, along with several chemical weapons facilities in the area. Viktor devoted most of his adult life to his work, only to lose everything when the Soviet Union collapsed.

"I hope the fucking Uzbeks choke on all that sand," Viktor exclaimed. "I heard half the fucking sea has dried up, so they can irrigate their dusty fields in the God-forsaken desert and grow more cotton for the fucking Chinese. I hope all the little fuckers are wearing

57

cheap underwear made with Uzbek cotton watered by the fucking dying Aral Sea. With any luck, some of the special stuff we cooked up on the island will find its way into the stinking water and into their fucking shorts."

Encouraged by a belly laugh from Boris, Viktor continued to rant, describing all the nasty diseases and crippling birth defects he hoped the Chinese would get from their cheap underwear made from (hopefully) poisoned Uzbek cotton.

When Viktor ran out of steam, Boris turned to business:

"Well, Viktor Viktorovitch, if you can satisfy my clients, as we discussed, you could retire to a villa on the Black Sea coast. I hear the government is encouraging retired army officers, like yourself, to buy property and settle in Abkazia, just to make sure the damn Georgians never get the place back. Are you ready to hit the road for a few months?"

Viktor nodded as he thought about Boris' invitation to accept a few months' work in Iran for $50,000 cash.

It would be a simple matter to teach a couple of foreigners to produce an anthrax weapon. He had seriously considered the offer, out of fear he would be forced to sell his comfortable apartment in the city just to buy the medicine he needed for his wife. But then, another opportunity came along, something that wouldn't require him to abandon his wife to struggle alone with her cancer.

"Boris, I simply can't travel right now. Svetlana is gravely ill and there's no one to care for her. As you know, our son died during the war in Chechnya, and his wife is a worthless piece of shit. Did I tell you she gave up our granddaughter for adoption to some fucking rich Canadians she met in Moscow, so she could buy some more fucking heroin?"

Boris didn't hide his disappointment. "Are you telling me I came all this way for nothing?" he asked, as he glowered at Viktor and pushed himself back from the table.

"Relax, Boris, relax! I've already prepared enough Anthrax to kill 10,000 assholes, in a powdered form that's easy to transport. You can have that today, if you want. In fact, you really must take it off my hands. More importantly, I've found something, or should I say someone better. Do you remember how you asked me to keep an eye out for talent, men with the kind of connections you need? Well, there's a fellow you need to meet..."

As Viktor drove Boris to his dacha hidden in the endless forest outside Novosibirsk, a pale sun set over a stark Siberian landscape. Viktor told Boris about his cousin, a Russian Army colonel with control over a dozen tactical nuclear warheads stored with his long-range artillery unit on the Chinese border. Some of the warheads were getting old and were scheduled for decommissioning, which presented an opportunity. It seems Viktor's cousin was ready to retire in style.

It was already dark when the two men arrived at Viktor's cottage, a traditional Russian structure made entirely of wood, with beautiful, decorative carvings around the windows. The night sky was clear and a full moon shone brightly when Viktor turned off his headlights and trudged through the snow toward the heavy wooden door.

The setting was beautiful, especially in winter. The cottage was surrounded by the kind of pristine Russian forest that would look strange to most Americans. All the trees were healthy, with no standing dead wood or fallen timber to be seen. The trunks were evenly spaced, like pillars in a cathedral, and the forest floor was uncluttered, with none of the underbrush that plagues many American forests. Russian peasants were self-sufficient and used every scrap of available wood, leaving nothing to waste. They took better care of their forests than many Americans took care of their cars.

Boris and Viktor took off their hats, jackets and boots in a narrow foyer. The house was already warm, with wood coals still glowing in a huge stove that stood in the middle of the house, with tile-covered bricks for retaining the heat and a large shelf above for sleeping on the coldest nights.

"I'd better put some more wood on the stove in the sauna," Viktor said as he shuttled off past the kitchen. Boris grunted in response as he sat by the stove to warm his hands and feet.

Viktor wanted the introductions to go well, so he made careful preparations. He covered the table with fresh brown bread, Siberian meat dumplings, pickled mushrooms and a half-dozen other "zakuski," or Russian appetizers. He also set aside several bottles of vodka which had been waiting all day on a shelf outside a window. The bottles were ice cold but had never seen the inside of a freezer. During the long Siberian winter, Viktor didn't need one.

The two men said very little and drank nothing until their guest arrived. Colonel Pyotr Ivanov was a robust-looking man, over six feet tall, with a broad chest and a full head of dark hair. He arrived alone, in civilian clothes, and parked a borrowed jeep just outside the door.

Viktor greeted his cousin warmly, in the Russian fashion, and introductions were made quickly and dismissed with. A bottle was opened as they gathered at the table and admired the feast that awaited them. No business was discussed as they downed toast after toast, with the vodka flowing into neat little glasses as fast as they could down them.

"Well, boys!" said Viktor, when he was sure his guests were well lubricated. "It's time for the sauna!"

It's a simple truth that most Russian men are unable to relax until they've had enough to drink. They'll arrive at a dinner, sullen and silent, until the drink flows freely and washes their reserve away. Once the bottle carries them to the desired destination, their personalities are transformed and the most cautious player may become a daring gambler. Russian men understand this about each other, so they never rush to discuss important business, as Americans will.

A Russian toga party is something to behold. All three men stripped and wrapped themselves in large, thin towels before stepping into the piping hot sauna. The space was cramped but the men barely noticed as they took turns pouring cups of water on red-hot stones, using a wooden ladle with a long handle.

"Did you hear the one," Pyotr began, "about the poor Ivan from Siberia, when he made his first trip to Moscow?"

"No," answered Viktor encouragingly. "Please tell us."

"It happened many years ago, when we were still boys." Pyotr continued. "Poor Ivan took the train all the way to Moscow and got drunk as soon as he could. Feeling his oats, and hoping to make an impression, he stumbled to the middle of Red Square. Angry at the closing of an old factory where he worked, poor Ivan shouted at the top of his voice: 'Brezhnev is an idiot!'"

"What happened then?" Boris asked enthusiastically, although he'd heard the joke before.

"He was arrested, of course," Pyotr responded, "and received a 20-year sentence; five years for insulting the leader of the Communist Party, and 15 for revealing a state secret!"

It didn't take much to get the men laughing as they finished their first bottle of vodka.

"So, how is the business in state secrets, these days?" Pyotr asked, directing his question at Boris.

"I'm retired, so I wouldn't know anything about state secrets!" Boris lied, pleased he wasn't the first to start the discussion. "But I can tell you, the money-making business is better than ever, for a man willing to take what he wants!"

"You boys stay here, while I get some more vodka," Viktor volunteered, leaving Boris and Pyotr to talk in private.

"Hum." Pyotr nodded his head as he tried to made up his mind. "Viktor tells me you're a respected businessman now, the kind of man who can put buyer and seller together."

"That's true, Pyotr, and I've got a serious buyer on the line, as we speak." Boris waited, to see if the colonel was willing to take specifics.

"Well then," Pyotor said, in a lower tone of voice. "What's the market these days for a pair of 1A62s?" The colonel waited, in turn, to see if the retired KGB man knew what he was talking about.

"Only two?" Boris asked, in mock surprise. Having done his homework, he knew the 1A62 was a tactical nuclear warhead, the kind maintained by Pyotr's artillery unit. "My clients are looking for at least four, at 10 million dollars a unit. But what about the fuses? Aren't they stored separately, under special lock and key? The 62's would be useless without them."

"Not to worry!" Viktor replied, thrilled to learn his merchandise was worth more than he expected. "I set aside two of the fuses last year, when they were officially retired from service, as soon as I learned the 62's were scheduled for decommissioning later this year. All of the merchandise is serviceable, by the way; a bit old, but still potent, just like us!"

The two Russian men shared a hearty laugh and slapped each other on the back as they negotiated a deal, with an option to purchase two more in six months, after the successful delivery and payment for the first pair. A few minutes later, Boris and Pyotr emerged from the sauna, in a jubilant mood, and joined Viktor at the table, still wrapped in their makeshift togas.

The highlight of the evening was a quick roll in the snow, commando style, before a final stretch in the sauna. The heat, the cold and the vodka dulled the pain in their aging bodies and made them feel young again, until the next morning.

Pyotr left at 10 a.m. after a parting toast with Boris. Like other Russian men, Pytor had been in training his entire adult life and his body could handle the vodka, at least until he died of a heart attack. He was sober as he drove back to town, with plenty of time to spare before catching a flight back to base.

Boris left later that morning with Viktor's anthrax packed carefully in his suitcase. The container weighed less than two pounds but could spread terror through an entire city.

Chapter 13: Free Enterprise

Flush with cash from higher oil prices and eager to flex its muscles, the government of Russian Prime Minister Vladimir Putin increased the budget of all its security agencies, including Russian military intelligence, the GRU. Anxious to show that his service could compete with Putin's former colleagues in the Foreign Intelligence Service (SVR) and the Federal Security Service (FSB), the external and internal successors of the KGB, the chief of the GRU invested most of his budget increase directly into overseas operations, with a secondary focus on recruiting and training new intelligence officers.

That was harder than the Kremlin realized, because the GRU only recruited from within the ranks of the armed services. Few of Russia's best and brightest sought a military career after the collapse of the Soviet Union. Why risk your life for a handful of rubles when you could work for a major corporation and live the good life in Moscow?

General Grigoriy Ivanovich Petrov, the son of a war veteran and factory worker who rose through the ranks on his own merit, was secretly pleased that he didn't have to recruit his officers from members of Moscow's increasingly prosperous elite.

Although he hid it well, there was nothing Petrov hated worse than the spoiled children of Moscow's Intelligentsia, the self-described intellectual class. He knew them well, having been married for a time to the daughter of a professor from the Moscow Institute of International Relations.

A brilliant but rough young man from a small military-industrial city, Petrov was never accepted by his wife's family and friends, even when he achieved rank and prestige within the service. No, Petrov had learned his lesson and would much rather recruit his officers from the hordes of hungry young men from the hinterlands, men without connection who wouldn't otherwise have an opportunity to get an education, to travel overseas or even to live in Moscow.

As General Petrov sat in his office and received a briefing on the GRU's latest successes against the Americans, one of the ambitious young men his service had recruited seized an opportunity, but not the kind of opportunity the General had in mind. The officer, a young lieutenant from a small mining town in the Ural Mountains, was responsible for supervising the transport of a truckload of secret documents from the GRU's crowded main building in Moscow to an archive at a small Russian Army base just outside the city.

While perusing his document inventory, the Lieutenant learned that one of the boxes included a set of files on the Metro systems of New York City and Washington, D.C. The Cold War era files were, in effect, professional casing reports for a possible Soviet "Spetznaz" (Special Forces) attack on both Metro systems. The files included full technical drawings of all the ventilation systems. The most detailed report described Metro stations near the Pentagon, with contingency plans calling for a surprise attack using anthrax spores. The executive summary of the report described how the plan could render the leadership of the formidable U.S. military ineffective for a few hours during a crisis, without direct attribution to the Soviet Union and without the need to use nuclear weapons, at least at first.

Unbeknownst to his superiors in the GRU, Lt. Pavel Tarasov had connections with the Russian mafia, some of whom were former members of the Soviet intelligence services. During a recent meeting with his mafia "Uncle," Tarasov was told he would earn some serious money if he could provide information on ports, railroad lines and highways in larger American cities.

Uncle Pavel explained the information was ostensibly needed by his corrupt American business partners. He said the greedy Americans wanted to gain an edge in the competition for U.S. government security contracts after the terrorist attacks in New York and Washington on 9/11, not to mention the billions of dollars being offered for infrastructure projects as part of an effort to stimulate the ailing American economy.

Uncle Pavel stressed the fact that Tarasov wouldn't be betraying Russia but would simply use his access in the GRU to collect information of potential business value to foreigners. Why should he worry about the Americans? They could take care of themselves, as far as Tarasov was concerned.

The energetic young Lieutenant had already collected information on the container port in Long Beach, California and received $4,000 in return, which was more than he made in a year. With another delivery, he figured he could earn enough to buy a used car, an absolute prerequisite if he ever wanted to spend some time with any of the beautiful women of Moscow, very few of whom were interested in wasting their youth on a penniless military officer, especially when the city was filled with rich foreigners and newly-rich Russian business-men.

It was easy for Lt. Tarasov to get rid of his driver, an enlisted man transporting him to the archives. All he had to do was time the trip to take place just before lunch hour, so they could stop along the way.

Wearing civilian clothes and sitting in the dark gray panel van he checked out from the GRU motor pool, Tarasov handed the man a few rubles and said:

"Corporal, why don't you grab a beer while I visit my girlfriend. She's a rich little cunt and won't shut up until I give her what she wants."

The corporal, a 20-year-old driver and mechanic, never missed an opportunity to avoid work. He quickly moved toward the door of a nasty-looking topless bar on the corner and shouted back over his shoulder, "Don't rush, Lieutenant, you'll find me right here when you're done!"

Leaning out the window on the driver's side of the van, Tarasov grinned and half saluted before heading south to meet Uncle Pavel at one of the new Lukoil petrol stations that were popping up everywhere in Moscow. It only took a moment to remove the American files from their carefully labeled box and to replace them with an equal number of old Red Army personnel files provided by Uncle Pavel. If anyone ever opened the file box again, which seemed unlikely, they would only assume the original documents had been misfiled.

Some things never changed after the collapse of the Soviet Union, especially the rule followed by every apparatchik; never be the first to report bad news up your chain of command. As a result, Lt. Tarasov was confident the files wouldn't be missed and if they were, no senior officer would find out. With $3,000 in crisp $100 bills in his pocket, the Lieutenant smiled to himself as the wheels turned inside his head. He made a personal vow to redouble his efforts to satisfy Uncle Pavel. He was young and the sky was the limit!

Chapter 14: Tools of the Devil

Ali Akbar Kalbasi sat quietly and gazed out the passenger window of an 18 wheeler as the heavily-laden truck rumbled along the road leading south through Iran from the Turkmen border. He had made dozens of successful border crossings for the Iranian Revolutionary Guard's elite paramilitary unit, the Quds Force, but this wasn't a routine trip. He was overseeing the transport of two weapons that could change the course of history.

He felt honored to be a part of his service's single most important operation, an action that would almost certainly drive the Americans from Iraq and enable his fellow Shia to carve out a friendly Islamic Republic along the border with Iran. The mission was an extremely personal one for Ali. He had lost many of his boyhood friends and suffered grievous wounds himself during the long, bloody war with Saddam's regime, a war his country had lost. If only the Shia of Iraq could achieve a final victory and carve out a new country for themselves, a country dependent on their brothers in Iran, all the old losses would be avenged and his life's work would be completed. Ali's sense of satisfaction was magnified by the knowledge that he was also serving a secret master, a man whose interests aligned perfectly with his own, his father's Russian friend.

The price the Russians extracted from Al-Qaeda was high, but well worth it. Ali's superiors in the Quds Force were more than pleased to facilitate the deal.

The exchange in Kazakhstan had gone as well as could be expected. The funds were transmitted to a secret Austrian bank account once Ali verified the weapons were genuine and the proper, coded text messages were exchanged by cell phone. Everyone thought Swiss banks were the standard of discretion, but Ali knew the banks in Vienna were better, if you knew how to make the proper arrangements.

At first, Ali was amazed when Boris Nikolayevich showed up for their meeting in the desert with nothing more than a driver and a small truck. Ali understood the situation better when his small team departed in their 18 wheeler and passed a heavily-armed convoy of dangerous-looking men on the road to the Turkmen border. That was no more than five minutes after they finished loading the crates and left Boris standing by the side of the road, smiling as he waved farewell to Ali.

Ali and his team had plenty of experience arranging clandestine shipments in Central Asia, using the same networks employed by local narcotics traffickers. With a little money in the right hands, all the paperwork was in order and the border crossings in and out of Turkmenistan were routine. Even if some local officials or lowly border guards suspected something was amiss, they could only assume the truck was transporting the usual contraband under the protection of a powerful mafia organization--definitely not a truck to trifle with.

There were a few technical obstacles, but Ali's superiors in the Quds Force, the elite paramilitary arm of the Iranian Revolutionary Guard, had taken care of that. The Iranians ran a very effective network of spies and agents of influence inside Turkmenistan. Once the Quds Force learned, with help from Boris and his Russian friends, that the Americans had given the government of Turkmenistan special radiation detection equipment for use at all border crossings with Iran, it was easy for Iranian operatives to make sure the detection station at one border crossing was down for maintenance at the appropriate time.

Ali remembered a lesson he learned during his many years as a successful Quds Force operative; no defensive security measures are capable of defeating a determined, well-informed enemy who has the time to make careful preparations. This lesson would hold true, even in the seemingly impregnable Green Zone.

Ali continued to sit quietly as the truck rumbled closer to the Iranian border with the Pakistani province of Baluchistan. Ali grew up in that region of Iran and spoke reasonably good Baluchi. His familiarity with the area made him a natural choice to serve as the primary liaison officer in Iran's extremely sensitive relationship with members of the Al-Qaeda terrorist network operating on the Pakistani side of the border.

The exchange with Usama Bin Laden's son Awwab took place on the outskirts of Zahedan, an Iranian border town on the main road to the Baluchi capitol of Quetta, in Pakistan. Awwab's wife and children lived in Zahedan, under the protection of the Quds Force, and Awwab crossed the border frequently, using an alias Pakistani passport provided by a Taliban sympathizer inside Pakistani military intelligence.

Two men were waiting as the 18-wheeler pulled up to the gate to a walled compound two blocks off the main highway in Zahedan. The wall was 18 feet high and encircled an area half the size of a football field, with two small buildings along the southern wall. As the airbrakes huffed and the truck came to a stop, Ali climbed down from the cab and was immediately greeting by Awwab, who emerged from one of the buildings with an armed escort provided by Ali's men. Already on good terms, Ali and Awwab embraced one other warmly:

"Asalam alekum," Awwab said with a broad smile.

"Alekum asalam," Ali responded, while holding the younger man by his shoulders.

"Are you ready?" Ali asked, looking directly at Awwab.

"If Allah wills it, we are ready," Awwab responded, lowering his dark eyes in mock deference to the older Iranian. His father had stressed the importance of staying in role, of allowing the arrogant Iranians to underestimate him.

"Good. I am the only one present, other than yourself, who knows what is really loaded in the two crates on this truck," Ali lied. "Both crates are labeled and papered over as 'medical equipment.' My men think we are transporting man-portable surface-to-air missiles for use by the brothers in Iraq. Three of those missiles are indeed loaded in the top of each crate, to conceal the special weapons underneath. I trust your security measures have been just as strict, as we agreed?" Ali asked.

"Yes, Ali, experienced men close to my father have made all of the arrangements. Thanks to your friends, the smugglers' route to Iraq is open. The sea route to America is also open. Both routes have been tried and tested. Only my father's most trusted men are involved, and all of them believe we are transporting missiles, for use in attacks against American aircraft, as we agreed. Only my father and his advisor know the truth."

"Good, good." Ali responded. "And what if we can deliver more of the same, in the future?"

"I'd have to talk to my father." Awwab responded cautiously. "I know he was disappointed we couldn't find three, to save one for the Zionists."

"Yes, of course. Please tell your father we may be able to help again, in the future." Ali wasn't sure if Boris would be able to get his hands on a third nuke, but he could try.

"Come then, let's rest and drink tea together before you depart for Quetta. How is your father, then?" Ali asked, as he walked with Awwab toward the small mud brick house.

Ali enjoyed a feeling of power when he met Awwab, not simply because he was older and more experienced, but also because he had successfully recruited a member of the young Arab's entourage. Ali's spy, a bright young man from Egypt who served as a special courier for the leadership of Al-Qaeda, was secretly a homosexual. Ali was amazed when he discovered this fact, with the help of a male prostitute on his payroll. The Egyptian was extremely cooperative, no doubt because he faced death and even worse, humiliation for himself and his family, if he was discovered by his Al-Qaeda colleagues.

All knowledge was power, but knowledge of the whereabouts of Usama Bin Laden was power indeed.

Chapter 15: A Needle in the Haystack

David Polansky glanced up at the clock above his desk as he rubbed his weary eyes. It was three in the morning and he still had several hours to go before the end of his shift at the National Security Agency's huge complex in Ft. Meade, Maryland.

David had volunteered for night duty because it eased the long commute from his condominium in Silver Spring, Maryland. David and his wife Amy had purchased the small apartment two years earlier, so she could be closer to her grueling job at the Walter Reed Medical Center, were she cared for wounded soldiers returning from the wars in Iraq and Afghanistan.

Amy's children from her first marriage were grown, so their move from a larger house in the Maryland suburbs made sense at the time. After commuting for more than an hour each way for the first 18 months after the move and then struggling to adjust his middle-aged body to a night shift over the past six months, David was having second thoughts. About a number of things.

The fact is, David and Amy were growing distant. That was hardly a surprise, since they rarely saw one other any more, at least not when both of them were awake. Not for the first time in his life, David yearned for a change, so he had spent the last 30 minutes scanning Department of Defense vacancy announcements, looking for an interesting position overseas.

Retrained as an Arabic linguist after the collapse of the former Soviet Union, when his mastery of the Russian language was no longer appreciated, David was in high demand. In fact, he could write his own ticket.

But should he? David had been through a bitter divorce many years before and he knew any decision to take an assignment overseas could lead to a permanent break with Amy.

That thought was too painful, so David decided to take another look at the documents on his desk, hoping the time would pass quickly so he could get home before Amy left for work.

David was a member of a small team tasked with looking for evidence of any contact between members of Al-Qaeda inside Pakistan and other members or supporters inside Iran. A series of vague but highly-classified human intelligence reports from the CIA's Clandestine Service suggested such contacts existed, so David and his team were tasked with finding supporting evidence and (hopefully) some actionable intelligence.

Transcripts of intercepted phone calls revealed a pattern of activity focused on Quetta, in the fiercely independent Pakistani province of Baluchistan. The intercepted calls were cryptic, with brief references to shipments of innocuous goods back and forth across the border with Iran and on to Iraq. Some of the participants in the telephone calls spoke Arabic with a Saudi accent, which made them a higher priority for intelligence collection. Unfortunately, David's targets changed phones regularly and his team had not succeeded in cobbling together anything of real intelligence value, at least not yet.

David had developed a special interest in one Saudi, a younger man who was treated with deference by his older telephone contacts. Or, David had to admit, he was interested in a series of younger, Saudi-accented voices that sounded to him like the same person using different names and telephone numbers. David's colleagues were skeptical and most didn't share his interest. Many of them had worked against narcotics traffickers for years, back when the long-forgotten "War on Drugs" was a top priority, and they recalled that ordinary criminals used multiple telephones with alias identities all the time. How could David be sure this particular Saudi was involved in anything of real interest, without hard evidence?

Yes, they could report with confidence the presence of Arabic-speaking Saudi men in Quetta, a city where the U.S. Government had no official presence and relied exclusively on the Pakistani government for help. And yes, David was confident these Arabs were involved in shipping goods back and forth from Pakistan to Iran. But what goods were they shipping? Foodstuffs and medical supplies, as they openly discussed over the telephone? Or perhaps narcotics needed to fund the Taliban's revival? Or possibly weapons and ammunition?

There simply wasn't any way for David to tell, not on his own, with only one source of intelligence to rely on. So David did what he always did; he drafted short intelligence reports documenting potentially suspicious activities and submitted those reports for release to the wider U.S. intelligence community, along with the tens of thousands of other raw intelligence reports flooding into massive data bases every day.

Surely, David thought, an all-source analyst at the National Counterterrorism Center will pull all those fragments together, if any of the names or telephone numbers in his reports overlapped with material from other sources.

At the same moment, on the far side of the world, a former Boston cop was working as a diplomatic security officer at the U.S. Consulate in Karachi, Pakistan. He was interviewing a man from Baluchistan who had waited in line for hours, ostensibly to apply for a visa to study in the United States, but in fact hoping to trade some information for hard cash.

The Baluchi, a handsome young man who called himself Ahmed, was amazed at the time and effort it took before he could actually speak with an American official. First, he had to get past the heavily-armed Pakistani soldiers who surrounded and protected the Consulate building. Then his passport and visa application were carefully scrutinized by an officious Pakistani policeman who looked him up and down in a disrespectful manner. After that, Ahmed had to work his way through a security checkpoint manned by local national employees of the American Consulate, complete with airport style x-ray scanners and metal detectors. Then, after cooling his heels for well over an hour in a crowded waiting room, Ahmed had to suffer through an initial interview with a Pakistani consular clerk who explained with a smirk that Ahmed would have to pay his visa application fee before his case could be reviewed by an American Consular officer:

"Oh, by the way, your fee won't be refunded if your application is rejected," the Pakistani clerk advised officiously.

Unbeknownst to Ahmed, the clerk worked secretly for Pakistani counterintelligence, as a penetration of the U.S. Consulate's local staff, all the better to keep a watchful eye on the Americans and potentially disloyal Pakistanis.

When Ahmed finally had a chance to speak with a busy American consular officer and explain that he wanted to talk to "an American security man," the Consular officer followed procedures and immediately contacted the office of the Consulate's Regional Security Officer to ask for assistance.

Brian Kelly, the officer who answered the phone, wasn't pleased. He was in the middle of drafting performance appraisals for the Consulate's huge local national security staff and didn't want to be interrupted. Besides, he had conducted similar interviews with more than 30 such "walk-ins" over the past month and all of them were a waste of time. Most of the men he interviewed were con artists of one form or another and the rest were simply crazy. Kelly also resented the fact that his section had to do so much of the grunt work for the CIA's base in Karachi, weeding out the worthless walk-ins so the glory-hogging CIA officers wouldn't have to waste their time.

By the time Ahmed had an opportunity to sit down, face-to-face, for a private conversation with Kelly, neither one of them was prepared for a pleasant conversation.

"So, Ahmed," Kelly asked bluntly, "what do you want?"

Already uncomfortable and in no mood to be insulted, Ahmed responded tersely, "I'm here to do America a favor."

"Right," Kelly responded. "I've heard that before. So, don't waste my time. Tell me exactly what you think it is you can do for America and what you want America to do for you."

Kelly had immediately categorized Ahmed as a likely information peddler, one of the hundreds of Pakistanis who tried to milk the consulate for money every year by pretending to have access to information of interest to the U.S. Government.

Ahmed squirmed in his seat and looked down at his feet for a moment before looking up again. He had gone to all this trouble to tell the Americans about some obnoxious Saudis living in his home town of Quetta, only to discover that the Americans were just as arrogant.

Finally, Ahmed continued:

"I need money to buy medicine for my father, who suffers from heart disease. If you help me buy the medicine, I will tell you about some Arabs who are living in Quetta. These Arabs are Wahabis, real fundamentalists, and I think they will be interesting to you."

Just as Kelly thought. Another information peddler. How predictable. They often tried to pull on a naive American's heartstrings, with tails of woe about their sick relatives and promises of providing valuable information about terrorists. The more grandiose fabricators tried to claim the multi-million dollar reward offered in exchange for information leading to the capture of Usama Bin Laden. The run-of-the mill fabricators, like this one, simply hoped to earn a few hundred dollars before slinking away into the stinking cesspool they called a city.

Before Kelly could decide what to do next, a large explosion rattled the Consulate's windows. In keeping with emergency procedures, Kelly unceremoniously escorted Ahmed back to the waiting room, where a large crowd mulled around in alarm. The Consular section was quickly evacuated by local security staff, while Kelly raced to the Consulate's main entrance to discuss the situation with the Marine guards on duty at Post One. When he arrived, the Marines were already wearing their emergency response gear. With more important things to worry about, Kelly quickly forgot about Ahmed.

For his part, Ahmed walked away from the building in disgust, avoiding the crowd of gawkers who gathered in hopes of catching a glimpse of the car bombing's aftermath. Angry and frustrated, Ahmed vowed he would never approach the Americans again.

He probably could have put the day behind him, if not for one thing he overlooked; his visa application was left in the hands of the Pakistani clerk, a man who was under orders from Pakistani counterintelligence to provide identifying information on anyone who was taken into the "back room" for private conversations with American officials like Kelly.

Later that evening, Ahmed's application was passed to a Pakistani intelligence officer and a special investigation was opened. Within 48 hours, Ahmed was picked up for questioning by a Pakistani internal security team. Unfortunately for Ahmed, the leader of the team was a Taliban sympathizer. A week later, Ahmed was reported missing. His body was never found.

Chapter 16: The Soul of a Stranger

Beirut, Lebanon - 1967

Martin McCrary was only 11 years old, but he could run like an antelope. He'd joined the junior track team at his private school in Beirut the year before, just for the training, so he could prepare for his escape.

Martin wasn't a slow learner, but it took him a few years to figure out what he had to do when he first arrived in Beirut. A stubborn streak seemed to run in the family and Martin was no exception. A small child when he arrived, Martin didn't like his situation one bit and he made sure everybody knew it.

The problem is, Martin was a stranger, and he didn't belong. His mother, the French-Lebanese entertainer Maria Sedari, dumped her son on an older sister, who wasn't pleased to have another mouth to feed. What was the point? Who wanted to raise a mongrel like that, the child of the disgraced Maria, pregnant and forced to marry a penniless foreigner, a petty criminal? Why should she have to bear the burden, while the boy's father sat in an American prison, unable to support his own son, and Maria lived the kind of life her sister would never know?

The beatings eventually broke Martin's stubborn streak, at least as far as anyone could tell, and he quickly learned to speak French at home and Arabic on the streets on the city. Even his aunt and uncle were impressed as they discovered Martin had a special gift for languages. Little did they know, the boy's greatest gift was acting, presenting the face he knew people wanted to see and saying the things he knew they wanted to hear, all with perfect sincerity.

When the time came, Martin was allowed to go to school, with tuition paid by his absentee Grandfather. The family had fallen on hard times after they lost everything in Havana, but Mr. Sedari was a tough old bastard and slowly worked his way back to prosperity, thanks to his American mafia connections.

In his secret soul, the soul of a stranger, Martin never felt at home in Beirut, and he was determined to find his father. He didn't know where home was, but he knew it wasn't in Lebanon. He hated the mother who abandoned him, and never wrote or visited him, but he loved the father who wanted him back, now that he was out of prison. Bad enough to come and get him.

And so it was that Martin found himself running down the long road to the sea, where his father waited. It was a cool night and he could see the lights shining in the harbor below, like a beacon for his heart. It seems Martin's father had some friends in the Merchant Marine, veterans of the Korean War, like himself, and they were able to arrange passage on a freighter bound for New Orleans, no questions asked.

Martin was quiet, for much of the voyage. His father, Billy McCrary, didn't have much to say, either, when he wasn't working in the galley, to help pay for the journey. The boy found it easier to talk to some of the sailors, family men who missed their own children and had more experience than Billy in dealing with a son. Martin watched his father carefully, however, and could see he was sharper and quicker than the others, especially at the card table.

After watching his father at work for several hours on a Sunday afternoon, he worked up his nerve and asked a question, in private: "Papa, why did you let them win?"

For a moment, Billy was speechless and more than a bit irritated. On the one hand, he was grateful to hear his son talking. On the other hand, he wondered how a boy could see what grown men couldn't.

"All right, son. I won't lie to you, so here's your answer. As I've gotten older, I've learned there's some things more important than money. Now, I owe these men a debt, for helping me get you home, so I let them win, more often than not, to pay them back a little, for what they've done." Billy put his hand, uncomfortably, on Martin's shoulder and waited to see if the boy had any more questions.

"If you can afford to lose, why not just pay them?" Martin asked the same impertinent questions when living with his mother's family and saw no reason to change now.

"They're too proud for that, son. You see, even work-a-day men like them need something to be proud of. These men, they don't have much, but they will help one of their own, when they can." That was the most Billy had ever said to his son, so he figured the conversation would stop there. It didn't.

"How'd you get out of jail, Papa? Did Grandpa come and rescue you, like you rescued me?" Even when he was a small child, Martin was always trying to walk in other people's shoes. Sometimes, when he was riding around in his uncle's car in Beirut, he would see a boy about his age, sweeping the sidewalk in front of a market, and wonder what that boy's life was like. He wanted to know what his Papa's life was like, too. Was he sad and lonely, like he was, when he was in jail?

Billy was angry, at the mention of his father, Big John McCrary. Martin, didn't know, of course, that his grandfather had testified against Billy, the first time he came up for parole. As a former deputy sheriff, Big John's word carried weight and he managed to delay Billy's release for years. Nor did young Martin see the letters sent by his grandfather, the ones warning the boy not to rejoin his father, the convicted felon and black sheep of the family. The letters were intercepted by Martin's Lebanese aunt, who forwarded them to Billy. She hoped Billy would take Martin off her hands as soon as possible, with no need for expensive legal proceedings.

As much as Billy loved his son, the best he was able, he never could control his temper.

"Your Grandpa is a bastard--and don't you forget it! You think your mother's family was bad--you ain't seen nothing! Now, don't you go sticking your nose where it don't belong--or I'll pack you off to live with that son of a bitch. That'd serve your right, you little shit!" Billy struck young Martin across the face with the back of his hand, but the blow hurt less than his words. Ashamed of himself, but too messed up to patch things up, Billy walked away in silence.

That was the day Martin began to understand a sad truth, a reality he first experienced during his childhood in Beirut. The world was populated by two kinds of people: those folks who made other people dance to their tune, like puppets on a string, and those folks who did the dancing. Right then and there, Martin took a solemn vow; he would make the bullies think he was the best dancer they had ever seen, while biding his time until he could dance them right off a cliff.

For the rest of his life, Martin never could abide a tyrant. He paid a high price for the impertinence, but really couldn't help himself, even if he'd wanted to.

Chapter 17: The Blue Danube

Martin rolled down the window of his Opal rental car as he drove south and east along the Danube River toward Vienna. He took a deep breath and slowed to a stop at a scenic overlook near the eastern end of the Wachau Valley. He had stopped at this location many times in the past so he could enjoy the view of the ancient castle at Durnstein, where Richard the Lionhearted was held for ransom during the Crusades.

His legs still stiff after the long flight from Mexico City, Martin climbed out of the car and walked over to the edge of the bluff to catch a better view of the river, which was brown and swollen from the Spring rains and a rush of melted snow from the mountains. Although eager to push on toward Vienna, where he hoped to see Fatima in a few hours, Martin willed himself to slow down, to take his time and think things through before venturing into the city he knew so well--well enough to know it could be dangerous.

It only took a few minutes for Martin to review his plan. He had taken a number of steps to avoid attracting attention. He began by driving across the border from Texas to the Mexican city of Monterey, where he caught a quick flight to Mexico City and a long connection to Munich.

Martin was traveling on a genuine Irish passport gained by virtue of his Irish grandparents. His great-grandfather, John McQuarie, was one of those rare Irish Presbyterians who supported Ireland's push for independence from Great Britain. John's father, William McQuarie, was a loyal British subject and a lifelong member of the Royal Irish Constabulary. The old man couldn't understand the anger and bitterness his son felt toward the English officers who led his friends to slaughter in the trenches of World War II. Years later, when the Irish Civil War turned nasty and John McQuarie barely escaped an attempt on his life, he fled with his wife and young children to America, where he built himself a new life in South Carolina.

As he examined his passport, Martin smiled at the generosity of the Irish, who welcomed back their lost sons, be they Catholic or Protestant. No one knew he had the document, which featured his great-grandfather's original spelling of the family name, all the better to foil prying eyes and databases.

Martin planned to pick up Fatima in Vienna and drive her back to a small riverside cottage, so they could spend some time alone. Everything was ready, including an emergency escape plan using a small inflatable raft he purchased during a short stop in Munich. Although he hoped Fatima would stay with him for a few days, he was prepared to drive her back and forth to Vienna, if necessary.

As Martin circled around a small shrine of the Virgin Mary, an ubiquitous sight on Austrian roadsides, a dark blur disturbed his peripheral vision. Glancing to his right, back toward the road, he saw a navy blue Volkswagen van speeding around a curve. The van appeared to slow down when the driver and passenger, two fit-looking men in their early 30's, found Martin's car parked at the overlook.

The passenger, a pale man wearing expensive sunglasses and three days of dark stubble, seemed to scan the area until he spotted Martin standing near the shrine.

In an instant, the man turned his head stiffly to the front, feigning disinterest while his lips moved rapidly. With considerable effort, the driver managed to avoid turning his head toward Martin in response, but not without rotating his eyeballs until they seemed to pop out of their sockets.

Martin was stunned. He had seen the same bad acting by surveillance teams many times in his career. Who in the hell was following him? How did they find him in Austria? What was he going to do now? He only had a few days to make contact with Fatima. If he failed, he might never see her again. Under normal circumstances, Martin would have aborted any planned meeting after determining he was under surveillance--but not today.

Martin walked quickly to the back of his rental car and opened the trunk. He grabbed his emergency bug-out bag, a small backpack with a few essentials, and threw the pack over his shoulders. Using both hands, Martin lifted a large nylon sack with the raft inside and worked his way down the slope to the river bank, abandoning his rental car. He opened the kit and used a footpump to inflate the boat in less than five minutes. The kit included a small, break-apart paddle and some safety gear. Martin threw all of his supplies into the raft, slid into the boat and pushed off the bank with his paddle. Within seconds, the raft was swept up by the current and carried downstream toward the ancient monastery at Krems.

With no bridge in either direction for miles, Martin only had to find a safe location to beach his raft on the far side of the river, around a bend and invisible from the road. Less than a kilometer downstream, Martin found just the right location near the village of Oberloin, one of the small communities scattered along the Danube's northern shore. After retrieving his backpack, Martin shoved the boat back out into the current so it would be carried further downstream, making it difficult for anyone to determine exactly where he left the water.

Climbing up the far bank, Martin found a taxi stand at a small commuter rail station and took the first of five taxi, bus, tram and metro rides before losing himself in the city. As always, Martin marveled at the reliability of Austria's public transportation network.

During a quick stop at a small clothing store in the working-class district of Ottakringer, Martin purchased one of the hats and blue cotton overalls worn by tens of thousands of craftsmen and laborers in Vienna. After donning his improvised disguise in a public restroom, he paid cash for two anonymous cell phones, with pre-paid minutes, from an ethnic Turkish street vendor. He thought briefly about acquiring some new, black-market identity documents, but decided to stick with his Irish passport because it was legitimate and he could travel just about anywhere in Europe, thanks to the EU's open internal borders.

Intimately familiar with the streets of Vienna from one of his first overseas assignments, Martin carefully checked for surveillance before arriving in the area of Mariam and Fatima's hotel, a comfortable tourist venue on the South side of town near the Schonbrunn Palace.

After watching the hotel from a nearby cafe, Martin walked briskly to the entrance and presented a small package, wrapped in festive paper and ribbons, to the female desk clerk. Speaking working-class German with a Slavic accent, Martin asked the clerk to deliver the package to Frau Khoury, the Lebanese-American businesswoman staying in the hotel, on behalf of a local antiques dealer. A few minutes later, a small box containing the anonymous cell phone was delivered to Mariam's hotel room door. When she opened the wrapping, she found a note from Martin inside.

"Dear Mariam," the note began. "I hope you and our mutual friend have arrived safely in Vienna. I can't tell you how grateful I am for everything you have done. Please open the box with the cell phone inside and follow the directions to activate it. I'll call you in 30 minutes, using the name Peter Hofbauer, a local antiques dealer. I know it may seem a bit awkward, but I need you to answer the phone. Please don't mention our friend's name or her native country, and don't forget to bring this note with you. I'll give you some directions that will require you to take public transportation, so please dress comfortably. Don't worry, even elegant ladies such as yourself ride the bus in Vienna, so you'll fit right in. I'll approach you when the time is right. See you soon, M."

90 minutes later, after receiving two calls from Martin and changing from a bus to a tram and back to a bus again, Mariam and Fatima arrived in the Viennese woods, a heavily-forested area surrounding the northern and western outskirts of the city. It was a cool spring day and the sun had already begun to set behind the hills when the bus reached its final stop. As instructed, Fatima and Mariam disembarked next to a small Heuriger, one of the rustic restaurants sprinkled around the village of Neustift-am-Walde.

Exhausted from their long flight and the unusual journey across Vienna, the two women stood quietly and looked for any sign of Martin. When the bus turned back toward the city, they crossed the narrow street and walked toward the entrance of the restaurant, an ancient, converted farm building nestled at the base of a steep hill, with newly-greening vineyards stretching behind stone walls as far as the eye could see.

At that moment, Martin emerged from the shadows to the left of the building and stood under a graceful arbor leading to the Heuriger's garden terrace. Mariam was the first to spot Martin; she gasped audibly and reached behind her to pull Fatima in his direction. Mariam stood quietly as the American and her Persian friend saw each other for the first time since their last walk together in Audubon Park, all those years ago.

Fighting back a rush of emotion, Martin stepped forward and searched Fatima's eyes before kissing her on both cheeks in the European fashion. Her eyes never left his until he turned to greet Mariam.

"Mariam, it's so good to see you. I regret all the trouble you've had to endure, but we had to protect Fatima. Come, I've reserved a table on the terrace. It's a bit early in the season, but we should be warm enough tonight."

"Well it's about time, Martin!" Mariam exclaimed, as she grabbed both of her friends by their arms as they walked thru the arbor gate. "I'm famished! But please don't order any of that awful green wine. The last time I drank at a Heuriger I had to nurse a savage headache all the way back to New Orleans!"

"As if that were anything new for you, Mariam! If I remember correctly, you always drank the boys under the table during Mardi Gras!"

With the tension released, the two Americans laughed and interrupted each other as they took their seats at an old oak table surrounded by low stone walls and topped with a vine-covered pergola. Fatima smiled and nodded her head from time to time but remained quiet. She couldn't help but think how different her life might have been if she had stayed in America when she was still young. But her father was determined to return to his native land, and if she hadn't married her husband, a powerful officer in the Revolutionary Guard, her father would have been imprisoned, or worse. Fatima yearned to make choices for herself, to enjoy the simple pleasure of pursuing her own happiness, without the burden of duty or responsibility.

Sensing her sadness, as his conversation with the more extroverted Mariam began to slow, Martin turned toward Fatima and smiled gently.

"Fatima, I can't believe it's you. There's a young man sitting inside me, trapped in this middle-aged body, looking out from under all this grey hair and he sees you sitting there, more beautiful than ever. I'm so glad you were able to meet Mariam. I hope it wasn't too difficult to get away."

"Martin, I see you've become an accomplished flatterer, at your advanced age," she teased. "Mariam told me you'd lost your youthful innocence, so I've been forewarned." Fatima smiled as she reached across the table to take his hand.

"But no," she continued, "the travel wasn't difficult to arrange, but it came with a price. I had to bring the wife of one of my husband's subordinates, so she can curry favor by purchasing gifts for her friends and relatives in Tehran. The men believe they have us under

93

control, but the young lady and I are the best of friends. She thinks I'll be out shopping and dining every day with Mariam, but I'll have to return to our shared room in a little pension near the Iranian embassy every night."

Martin tried not to show his disappointment. He didn't want to push Fatima, but realizing time could be short, he tried to move the conversation in a critical direction.

"So, you'll be going home, then?" he asked quietly, while still holding her hand.

Fatima glanced over at Mariam and lowered her eyes as her Lebanese friend rose from the table.

"I hope the two of you don't mind if I take a walk in the vineyard. Martin, Fatima knows she can come home with me, if she wants. I have plenty of room and could easily put her to work in one of my businesses." Mariam stood looking at Fatima and Martin for a moment before she turned and walked up a stone path toward the gentle hill behind them.

"Fatima, I know it will be hard for you, but I think you should accept Mariam's offer. She told me about your son; I was so sorry to hear about his accident. But you're free to leave Iran now, there's nothing holding you back. You deserve a chance to live a real life, a life of your own, and I think I may be able to help you stay safe."

Tears welled up in Fatima's eyes as she thought about the empty years since her son had died in a freak accident at school. A talented young gymnast, he had suffered a fall that broke his neck and ended his life prematurely. After that, her already-strained relationship with her husband was worse than ever and the beatings began. She looked up at Martin, ready to leave all of her bad memories behind in Tehran, but then she remembered why she had reached out to Martin in the first place.

"Martin, before I can decide what to do with my insignificant life, before I can have any hope for the future, I need to tell you something, something important. I think my husband and his compatriots are planning some kind of attack, something they believe will drive the U.S. out of Iraq and Afghanistan very quickly, not in victory, but in defeat. After all the unrest following the election, they're worried and want to unite the country against a foreign enemy again."

It was more difficult than usual for Martin to push his emotions aside. With considerable effort, he adopted his professional persona and listened carefully as Fatima described the conversation she overheard, on an evening when her husband hosted Brigadier General Suleimani for a meeting at home.

Fatima explained how she fell asleep at around 11 that evening, but rose a few hours later when she heard voices in her husband's study. She found it strange, since her husband usually went to bed by midnight, so she pressed her ear to the door and listened.

"What did your husband say?" Martin asked.

"Not much, at first," she responded. "He was listening while the General talked. The General told him President Ahmadinejad was counting on the success of their operation. He joked with my husband and said the Americans would no longer be able to hide behind the walls of their embassy in the Green Zone, since there wouldn't be a Green Zone any more."

"That does sound serious, Fatima, what else did you hear?"

"I'm afraid I missed a great deal, but my husband did ask the General a question. He wanted to know how they could trust the Arabs and the Russians."

"How did the General respond?"

"The General lowered his voice and seemed to be giving my husband orders. The tone of his voice was very severe, and yes, I remember him saying there were several reasons why he could rely on the Arabs, even if he didn't trust them."

"First, the General said he was giving Al-Qaeda something they could never acquire on their own, special weapons he called the 'Zulfiqar' that would drive remaining American forces out of Iraq forever. Al-Qaeda would get credit for that, he said, a motivation the Sunni group's egotistical leaders wouldn't be able to resist."

"What exactly does 'Zulfiqar' mean, Fatima? Do you know what kind of weapon it might be?" Although Martin spoke decent Arabic and some Persian, he didn't recognize the word.

"It's an important sword, in the Koran," Fatima answered. "My husband has used the word several times before. He's a 'Twelver', you know, just like President Ahmadinejad." Fatima paused to see if Martin understood the implications.

"Oh, of course, now I remember!" Martin responded. "The Twelvers believe the 12th Imam, the Mahdi, will return at the Day of Judgement, to institute a kingdom of justice and to fight alongside Jesus against the Antichrist." Martin was dismayed by the similarities

96

between the End Times prophecies of Islam and Christianity and had learned what he could from one of his knowledgeable colleagues. "But what exactly is the Zulfiqar, what's the significance?" Martin asked.

"My father told me the story, when I was still quite young. The Zulfiqar belonged to the Prophet Mohammad. According to tradition, it was a powerful scimitar, with two v-shaped points at the tip. The Prophet gave the sword to his cousin and most faithful companion, Ali, to recognize his courage. Later, Ali's son, Husayn bin Ali, who was also the Prophet's grandson, carried the sword when he was martyred at the Battle of Karbala, in Iraq. That's where the schism between Sunni and Shia Islam began. The Twelvers, like my husband, believe the Mahdi, the 12th or Hidden Imam, will carry the sword of the Prophet when he returns at the End Times."

"Wait a minute, now I remember. Didn't Ali marry the Prophet's daughter, Fatima?" Martin asked.

"Yes, that's right. My mother named me after her. She was more religious than my father." Fatima tried not to dwell on the sense of sadness she felt at the memory of her mother, who passed away when she was a girl.

Martin sensed Fatima's discomfort and pressed on. "Okay, now I'm beginning to understand. The name 'Zulfiqar' was important in the history of Islam, so your husband and the General are using it as a code name-- but for what? Do you have any idea what kind of weapons they were talking about?"

"I don't know Martin, but I fear they may be nuclear bombs, because the General said the 'Zulfiqar' would also be used to 'melt' Wall Street, an attack that was guaranteed to 'destroy the enemy's weak economy and render him impotent.' Apparently there was a debate within Al-Qaeda and some of them wanted to launch a simultaneous attack against the Israelis, too. The General also described the weapon as the 'fire of Allah.' Yes, those were his words when he spoke to my husband."

"And there was more," Fatima continued. "The General reminded my husband that their subordinates had discovered the location of Usama Bin Laden and many of his senior advisors, which the General planned to leak to the Americans immediately after the attacks by Al-Qaeda. When the dust settled after the expected retaliation by the Americans, the General said he believed the leadership of the remaining Sunni insurgency in Iraq would be too weak to oppose Iran's Shia allies. The General also predicted the Taliban would no longer have a realistic chance of seizing power again in Afghanistan, leaving Iranian surrogates to dominate both of Iran's neighbors."

Martin sat for a moment, stunned by the implications of what he just heard, his head spinning with unanswered questions. "Was there anything else, Fatima? Did the General explain what he meant when he said the weapon would 'melt' Wall Street and make the Green Zone disappear? Did they say anything else about an Israeli target? And what about the Russians? How are they involved?"

"No, Martin, I'm ashamed to tell the truth. I was so frightened by my husband's words, so afraid he would find me at the door, I fled to my bedroom and pretended to sleep. I'm sorry, I failed you."

"No, Fatima, No--I'm the one who should be ashamed. You've shown so much courage, you've risked everything by contacting me, by coming here. Mariam mentioned your troubles at home and I believe your life is in danger. You've done everything anyone could expect of you, so let me share the burden."

"You should think of your future," Martin continued. "Have you considered Mariam's offer? You'd be safe, and once I've done what needs to be done, I'll find you."

Before Fatima could raise her eyes to respond, Mariam returned and took her seat at the table. By mutual, unspoken agreement, they spent the next hour enjoying a meal together. They talked about family and friends, passions and interests, while avoiding sensitive topics.

When the meal was finished, they called a taxi and rode back to the hotel, sitting silently as they sped through the hills toward the lights below. Fatima sat in the middle of the back seat, with her right side pressed against Martin and his left hand clasped in her lap. Exhausted physically and emotionally, she was sustained by a sense of peace she had not known since the day her son was born.

When they reached the plaza in front of the hotel, Mariam smiled and said, "Why don't the two of you go up and visit for a while? I'm not tired, and if I hurry, I can still make the last act of the 'Magic Flute' at the Volksopera."

Fatima turned to her old friend and thanked her silently, with a kiss on the cheek as she slid out of the taxi behind Martin.

"I'll be back at midnight, Fatima. I hope you'll still be here when I return!" Mariam smiled but looked a bit worried as she sped away, leaving her friends alone by the curb.

"Would you like to join me for a cup of coffee?" Martin suggested.

Fatima turned to face Martin and took both of his hands in hers. Smiling and looking directly into his eyes, she said:

"You haven't changed that much, have you Martin. You're still the kindest man I've ever known. But no, I don't want a cup of coffee."

As she spoke those words, Fatima placed the key to Mariam's hotel suite in Martin's hands as she led him through the lobby toward the elevator.

When they got to the spacious room, there was nothing left to say, at least not yet. The three hours they spent alone together seemed to last forever, until it was over and seemed to vanish like a dream upon awakening. But for a time, the world stopped turning and the couple renewed a love that had never grown past the Spring of their youth, never faded and never grown cold. Martin was the generous lover Fatima had never known. As she lay by his side, feeling spent but alive, without guilt or remorse, she made up her mind. She would leave everything behind and love Martin for the rest of her life.

Searching his eyes as they lay side by side, Fatima placed her hand on Martin's cheek and asked him to take her back with him to America. Overcome with emotion, the couple shared tears of joy as they held each other close.

"Fatima, there's so much we have to do," Martin said, as he rose from the bed. It's too dangerous for you to stay here past morning. There's too much risk your young friend will run straight to the Iranian Embassy in the morning, to report you as a missing person. We'll have to move you to a safer place, while I make some arrangements. You can't just show up at the airport with an Iranian passport and catch a flight to the States."

"I'll need to speak to some people at the American Embassy," Martin explained. "They'll want to talk to you in person, about your husband and the General, and it may take a few days before they're satisfied. There's a very good chance you'll be given special treatment, which will smooth your entry into the country. It won't be easy at first, Fatima, but when the storm has passed you'll be able to live in peace."

Shortly before midnight, Mariam returned to her room. She seemed thrilled to hear the news about Fatima's plans and promised to do everything she could to help. Reluctant to part, Martin and Fatima took a long walk in a quiet neighborhood surrounding the hotel, making arrangements for the following day. As they strode hand in hand down a narrow, cobblestone alley, Martin revealed for the first time his affiliation with the CIA. Although she wasn't surprised, Fatima expressed considerable relief when she learned Martin was planning to retire as soon as he could.

At that moment, two Mercedes sedans emerged from either end of the short alley. Six men speaking a language Martin didn't understand rushed toward the couple. The unarmed American stepped forward, with his hands in plain sight, sizing up the situation.

"Who are you, what do you want?" Martin asked in German.

The oldest member of the group, a short, stocky man with close-cropped gray hair, answered in English: "Your cooperation, of course."

As he spoke, three of the men drew concealed handguns and trained them on Martin. One man stood behind him and two on either side of their leader.

"We don't want to hurt either one of you," the older man continued, "but you must do as I say."

Martin moved a few steps closer to the leader, to test the group's reaction. Unlike a scene in the movies, armed professionals never allow a victim to get close enough to gain control over their weapons. At that moment, two fit-looking young men stepped around their armed colleagues and rushed toward Martin. As he prepared to defend himself, he was hit with a taser and fell immediately to the ground, rolling and twisting on the pavement. Unable to control his own body, he watched helplessly as the group forced Fatima into one of their sedans and sped away. Struggling to right himself, Martin was tasered again and lost consciousness.

Sometime later, Martin woke up and found himself strapped to a gurney inside an ambulance, which shook violently as it bounced along a rough country road toward the Austrian border with Slovakia.

Chapter 18: The High Seas

The Atlantic Commerce, a container ship owned by a Dutch multi-national corporation, was registered in the West African country of Liberia to keep taxes and regulations to a minimum. There were hidden costs, to be sure, but the bribes the company paid to certain Liberian government officials added up to far less than the cost of a European or American registration.

The Atlantic Commerce had an experienced Dutch Captain, but most of the crew hailed from Asia. An outspoken atheist, the Captain had no idea the ship's cook was a Muslim fighter from the island of Mindanao, in the Philippines. Born a Muslim in a country dominated by a Catholic majority, the cook had been carefully trained to play the role of a docile Filipino Christian. He carried genuine papers, which were issued by a corrupt government official in the capitol city of Manila, using a common Filipino Christian name: Fernando Cruz.

The cook, a martial arts expert known as Abu Assam by his fellow mujahidin, found it easy to impersonate a Catholic. Both of his parents were killed during a Philippine Army raid on his small village on the island of Mindanao, using weapons, equipment and training provided by the U.S. Army. After the raid, a senior Filipino officer who once studied for the priesthood delivered all of the surviving children to a Catholic orphanage in Davao City, where they were "converted."

Abu Assam, a small but determined boy who never forgot the faith of his fathers, escaped by boat to Indonesia when he was a teenager. After training in a series of camps operated by Indonesian extremists, Abu

Assam found himself fighting alongside Usama Bin Laden and other foreign fighters during the great jihad against the godless Soviet Army in Afghanistan.

Later, Abu Assam swore an oath of loyalty to Bin Laden, whose lieutenants recognized the value of his fluent English and his ability to pose as a Christian. By then, the leadership of Al-Qaeda had also learned that thousands of Filipino workers were employed at U.S. embassies and military bases around the world.

During a port call in Hong Kong in the winter of 2007, Abu Assam met with a special representative of Al-Qaeda, a soft-spoken Libyan who asked him to collect information on security procedures at American ports, to support an important operation. By the winter of 2008, Abu Assam had visited half a dozen U.S. ports, while exceeding the expectations of his superiors in the quality and quantity of information he was able to provide.

An experienced operative, Abu Assam was honored by the trust placed in him. He was determined to make sure the Stinger missiles concealed aboard his ship arrived safely at their destination in America. He was told the missiles would be used in a coordinated attack against several major American airports, as part of a broader effort to destroy the American economy, which was already mired in a recession.

He understood the argument presented by the Libyan, who explained how the attack would drive the Americans from Iraq and Afghanistan because they wouldn't be able to afford the cost. God willing, the Libyan said, America would eventually withdraw behind its borders, as all of the great European powers had done when their empires collapsed. When that happened, there would be no one left to protect the tyrants and col-laborators ruling so much of the Islamic world, and they would be swept away.

Abu Assam reviewed his plan as he enjoyed some fresh air on the afterdeck. The missiles were hidden in a crate, which in turn was concealed in an anonymous container from Hong Kong. The crate was the same size as many other crates sealed in the container, which was documented as a shipment of transformers needed for a new electrical substation somewhere in America.

During his travels, Abu Assam had learned that se-curity was heaviest at the largest American ports located near military bases or important federal government fa-cilities. Smaller cities, especially those lacking an FBI field office, were less secure. He was amazed when he discovered this useful fact simply by consulting local telephone books.

With Abu Assam's help and a little effort, Al-Qaeda operatives were able to route the special ship-ment through one of the least secure ports on the south-eastern coast of the United States. Since only a small percentage of containers were ever opened, there was very little chance the missiles would be discovered. If the crate was opened by anyone other than the intended recipient, it was rigged to explode immediately, which would destroy the evidence and serve as a useful diver-sion in its own right.

Abu Assam didn't know how the crate would be handled by other Al-Qaeda operatives already on the ground in the United States, but he was assured every-thing was ready. He had volunteered for the special training needed to operate the Stinger missiles himself, since he could easily slip away once his ship arrived in

America, but the Libyan told him his valuable services were needed elsewhere.

Although Abu Assam longed for martyrdom, he was content to wait. In two days, his ship would reach America and he would be free to accept another assignment.

Unbeknownst to Abu Assam, he wasn't the only Filipino Muslim working for the Libyan Al-Qaeda operative. His organization had also penetrated the seemingly impregnable Green Zone in Baghdad, using two Filipino men with backgrounds remarkably similar to Abu Assam's. A major U.S. defense contractor was more than eager to hire the men because they were willing to take the low-paying jobs no self-respecting American would accept. A bustling city within a city, the Green Zone produced a lot of garbage, and somebody had to drive the trucks.

Chapter 19: Sacrifice

The little American boy stood at the railing of a crowded passenger ship, shielding his eyes from the Caribbean sun. He could see Carmelita standing by the landing, perfectly still, with her right hand clutching her heart and her left hand lifted high, reaching for him. The scene behind her was chaotic, as thousands of men, women and children milled about in panic, stumbling over their belongings, unable to afford passage out of Havana or lacking the connections needed to get on that ship. As the boy reached for his nanny he fell over the side and plunged into the clear water below. He felt her warm embrace as the water enveloped him. Her smiling face sparkled in the surface of the water above as he sank to the bottom and slowly closed his eyes.

When Martin woke from his dream, he was still strapped down, but this time he found himself in the dark cellar of an old masonry building. Two bright florescent lights hung directly overhead, making it difficult for Martin to focus his eyes. Hearing muffled voices nearby, Martin tried to speak:

"Where's Fatima?" he croaked, through parched lips.

The muffled voices continued for several minutes until Martin heard footsteps moving in his direction. Looking up, he saw the shadow and then the outline of a face, an older man with dark hair and wire-rimmed glasses.

"Don't worry, Martin, she's safe and sound. In fact, she'll soon be back home in Tehran. She told us everything we needed to know, about her husband, and didn't object when we explained the situation." The man spoke English with an accent Martin found difficult to place.

"What situation, what are you talking about?" Martin asked.

"Why you, of course," the man explained. "We told her we'll keep you safe until she completes the task we've assigned. How could we possibly allow her to defect, when there's so much she could do to help us? She's a reasonable woman and accepted our proposal immediately."

"Who the hell are you and where the hell are we?" Martin wanted to know.

"Well, you're being held in a very private facility in Eastern Europe, not far from the Austrian border. My organization has a special relationship with the locals-- they're very helpful. When I told them we needed to question a suspected terrorist, they were more than will- ing to accommodate us."

"I don't understand," Martin complained. "What in the hell do you expect to gain by holding me?"

"I think you understand very well, Martin. But the time for questions is over. It's time for answers. First, you're going to tell me everything you know about Fatima's husband and his boss, General Suleimani, just to make sure we got everything right. Then, you're going to tell me again."

"If you cooperate, we'll help Fatima escape Iran, once she's done what we've asked her to do. We'll also release you, as we promised your lovely Persian friend. If you refuse to cooperate, Fatima will have to remain with her husband in Tehran. I'm sure you'll agree that wouldn't be fair to her."

Martin tried to figure out who was holding him. Could it be the Russians? Their ties with the Slovaks were historically close, and they had plenty of reason to be interested in Fatima's story. Did the man's accent give him away? Martin couldn't place it, but he had known many intelligence officers whose first language was different from the country they served. What about the Israelis? They were very active in Vienna and had more reason than anyone to worry about terrorist attacks using weapons of mass destruction. It didn't take long for Martin to review his options.

"Of course, I'll do whatever it takes to help Fatima. But first you should know I'm retired from my previous employment and I have no interest in Iran beyond her."

"Well, there may be some truth in that statement, Martin. But that does make your Irish passport difficult to explain, doesn't it? Okay, let's start with the easy part."

At that point, the faceless man began to question Martin about his relationship with Fatima. He wanted to know everything there was to know, and he took careful notes.

The following morning, Martin's inquisitor sat in his office at the Israeli Embassy in Vienna. The most senior Mossad officer in Europe, Ephraim Kodar had a serious problem on his hands. He knew his superiors would never support his decision to detain an American citizen, much less a retired CIA officer.

"So, what are we going to tell Headquarters?" David Glassman, Ephraim's talented deputy, was worried. He knew his career was also on the line, if his boss made the wrong call.

Ephraim wasn't in the habit of withholding information from his superiors, but this situation was different and he needed to buy some time.

"In two days," Ephraim reflected, "the woman will return to Tehran, and there's nothing the American can do about it. After that, we'll 'discover' the true identity of our mysterious Irishman, them we can release him, no harm done."

"Surely he'll run straight to the CIA in Vienna and tell them the whole story?" Glassman suggested.

"I doubt it," Ephraim explained. "I'm convinced he's been playing out of bounds. He could easily find himself in trouble, if he shows up at the American embassy. Besides, the Iranian plot will be in the news soon enough. After that, he won't feel obligated to relay the story himself."

"What do you mean?" the deputy asked, with genuine surprise. "Why would anyone leak our report? We haven't even written it yet!"

"Don't be naive," Ephraim responded gruffly. "This is the opportunity we've been waiting for, a chance to stop the Iranians, before they can develop nukes of their own! So, the answer to your question is simple; our bosses will share the information with the U.S. Government, and one of our American friends will leak it. You can count on it."

"So, the woman is expendable?" the deputy asked, with a hint of the criticism that question implied.

110

"We're all expendable, and don't you forget it!" Ephraim barked.

David didn't like it, but Ephraim's logic was impeccable. Protecting the country came first. Everything else came last.

"I understand and support your decision," the Deputy responded. I'll get to work on that report." Ephraim didn't bother to acknowledge the younger man as he left his office.

Based on his conversations with the American and his initial debriefing with Fatima, Ephraim was convinced the terrorists had somehow gotten their hands on two nuclear weapons, maybe three; what else could the Iranians have meant when they said Al-Qaeda was planning to "melt Wall Street" and "destroy the Green Zone?" The veteran intelligence officer was frustrated by the lack of detail on a possible attack against Israel. Even one nuke could devastate his small country. He had to collect more information, and Fatima was his only chance.

The plan was risky, but Ephraim knew exactly what he had to do. He would report back to Tel Aviv that his trusted agent, Mariam Khoury, had successfully brokered an introduction to her Persian friend, Fatima Lavasani. He would confirm the targeting team's analysis that Fatima was the wife of Quds Force Colonel Sattar Fakoor, an infamous enemy of Israeli who was directly involved in providing support to Hezbollah and Hamas. He knew his superiors would be pleased to learn the Colonel was reporting directly to the Quds force Commander, General Suleimani.

Ephraim also planned to submit an intelligence report, which he knew would be released to the American government, outlining Iran's involvement in allowing Al-Qaeda to get its hands on weapons of mass destruction.

Everything else was predictable. The Obama administration would be forced to abandon its plans for direct talks with the Government of Iran. The pressure to launch a retaliatory attack on Tehran would be overwhelming. Such an attack would lead to significant delays in Iran's secret nuclear weapons program. Perhaps the delays would be long enough to allow Israel, with support from its allies in the United States, to engineer a change of regime in the Islamic Republic. With the immediate threat from Iran removed by the Americans, and with the panic surrounding fears of a terrorist attack using nuclear weapons, Israel would be free to deal with Hezbollah and Hamas, once and for all.

Ephraim was a hard man. He believed it was a dangerous waste of time to talk "peace" with terrorists.

Chapter 20: Compelling Evidence

Steve Campbell, the senior officer on duty at the National Counterterrorism Center in Mclean, Virginia choked on his coffee when he read the latest report submitted by the CIA's station chief in Israel.

"Holy shit!" He sputtered at his exhausted colleagues sharing the graveyard shift. "Somebody get the boss on the line--we're gonna have to wake him up for this one!"

The report was marked URGENT - TOP SECRET and had been presented to the CIA's Chief of Station in Tel Aviv early that morning during a rare personal meeting with the Director of Mossad, Israel's foreign intelligence service, and the Chief of Shin Bet, Israel's internal security service. As the rest of his colleagues scrambled to notify senior Agency officers on their call list, Steve printed out a copy of the report so he could read it more carefully.

Steve spent most of his days in front of a computer screen, but somehow the hundreds of raw intelligence reports he read every day seemed more substantive when he could hold the most important ones in his hands. This report was spectacular, but thin on detail:

SUBJECT: IRANIAN INVOLVEMENT IN AL-QAEDA PLOT TO USE WEAPONS OF MASS DESTRUCTION

SENIOR OFFICIALS OF THE IRANIAN REVOLUTIONARY GUARD CORPS (IRGC) ARE FACILITATING THE TRANSFER OF PROBABLE WEAPONS OF MASS DESTRUCTION FROM UNKNOWN SOURCES IN RUSSIA

TO MEMBERS OF AL-QAEDA BASED IN PAKISTAN. THE WEAPONS, CODE NAMED "ZULFIQAR" (THE SWORD OF THE PROPHET), WERE TO BE USED BY AL-QAEDA FOR SIMULTANEOUS ATTACKS ON THE U.S. EMBASSY AND THE GREEN ZONE IN BAGHDAD AND ON WALL STREET IN NEW YORK. UNKNOWN ISRAELI TARGETS WERE ALSO BEING CONSIDERED. THE SENIOR IRGC OFFICIALS HOPED THE ATTACKS WOULD FORCE THE U.S. TO WITHDRAW ITS REMAINING FORCES FROM IRAQ, SETTING THE STAGE FOR A TAKEOVER BY IRAN'S IRAQI SHIA SURROGATES.

Steve was thunderstruck. How on earth could he release such a spectacular, potentially irresponsible report without knowing more about the source, without being able to offer some context, to help senior intelligence officials and policymakers evaluate the information? He took a close look at some notes submitted by the Chief of Station, an experienced officer who immediately understood the firestorm the report would unleash when it hit the streets in Washington. According to the Chief, the Director of the Mossad personally vouched for the information. He claimed his service had an active source and expected to collect additional information over the next few weeks.

Steve had been around the block, and knew what the report would mean:

"Well, boys and girls, it looks like we may be going to war with Iran. Buckle your seat belts and get cranking; we have to task every source we have, human or technical, to see if we can find anything to verify this report."

As Steve settled in to write a dozen e-mails to key players in the intelligence community, to ensure the report was included in the President's daily briefing, he felt uneasy. He knew at least some portion of the report would be leaked to the press within days to help make the case for war with Iran. There were just too many players in Washington who already opposed President Obama's plans to negotiate with the Iranians, including senior members of the Republican Party who were eager to portray the Democratic administration as "soft" on terrorism. Steve was surprised at how short Obama's "honeymoon" had been, as the Republican Party moved aggressively to regain its footing after a bitter electoral defeat in the fall of 2008.

If the Israelis really do have an agent on the ground in Tehran, he won't last long, Steve thought to himself.

Chapter 21: Homeward Bound

As Fatima sat in the international airport outside Vienna, waiting to catch her flight back to Tehran, she tried to calm herself. Her young friend sat by her side and talked excitedly about all the fine things she purchased during her shopping expedition. Feigning interest, Fatima smiled and nodded as her friend removed various items of clothing from her shopping bags and held them up for Fatima to admire.

Out of the corner of her eye, some movement caught Fatima's attention. A large crowd was gathering near a television suspended from the ceiling, on the opposite side of the waiting area. Several men in the crowd were Iranian citizens, like herself, and she saw one of them pointing at the screen while shouting something about "American propaganda" in Farsi.

Alarmed, Fatima stood up and walked over toward the crowd, leaving her young friend behind. She edged closer to the crowd and asked, "What is it?"

"Shhh! Be quiet and listen!" an older Persian man hissed.

The television was tuned to Fox News and the commentator, Bill O'Reilly, was reading from his teleprompter:

"This news just in. Unnamed sources in the Pentagon claim they have firm evidence the Government of Iran has provided unspecified weapons of mass destruction, or WMD, to terrorists operating in Iraq and Afghanistan, including Al-Qaeda. WMD is shorthand for nuclear, chemical or biological weapons. According to sources on Capitol Hill, senior figures in the Republican

Party plan to hold a news conference this evening to demand more information from the administration and to condemn President Obama's planned meeting with Iranian President Amadinejad at the United Nations next month."

The screen flickered briefly and a panel of conservative and liberal "experts" appeared, with each talking head framed in its own box while O'Reilly fanned the flames. Richard Perle, one of the architects of the Iraq war, was the most assertive:

"My sources tell me this is the real deal," he exclaimed. "We're talking about hard, unshakable evidence that Iran is providing support to Al-Qaeda, with the goal of driving remaining U.S. forces from Iraq in defeat and humiliation. This has serious implications. All of those liberals in the Obama administration who think we should negotiate with Iran will be forced to eat their words. Any reasonable person has to agree; the provision of material support to a terrorist organization involved in attacks against the United States is nothing less than an act of war."

The panel quickly deteriorated into a shouting match, with a Democratic spokesman accusing the Republican Party of orchestrating a disinformation campaign like the WMD debacle that was used to justify the invasion of Iraq.

Feeling faint, Fatima stumbled backward and reached behind her to find a seat. She covered her face with her hands and lowered her head to her lap for a moment, until the feeling passed. Fatima's young Persian friend rushed over and put her arm around her shoulders.

"You look pale, Fatima, are you all right?"

"Yes, yes, I'll be fine. I'm getting older, you know, and I'm not used to traveling. I'll be fine in a moment."

"Don't worry," the young woman assured her. We'll be safe at home in a few hours."

That was no comfort for Fatima, of course. She knew she was involved in something far greater than herself, and for the first time, she realized she might not survive. At least she could try to help Martin: she had no other choice.

Chapter 22: The Tutor

New Orleans, Louisiana - 1978

Martin McCrary met his tutor at a chess tournament hosted by Tulane, during a friendly competition with students from Loyola University in New Orleans. The team from Loyola was the best in the city, thanks to their teacher, Father Paul. The good Father was a Jesuit and a professor of philosophy; he was also a well-connected native with a Cajun background. He had a mind as quick as an alligator's bite and the self-discipline to match.

Martin lost his match that day to the best student on Father Paul's team, but the game was a close one. Father Paul must have seen something he liked because he took a special interest in Martin after that.

"Very impressive, Martin," Father Paul began, as the students and professors mingled after the match. "Your faculty advisor told me you have a keen intellect. Can I interest you in some private lessons?"

Surprised and flattered, Martin wanted to say yes, but he knew he would have to reject the offer, for the same reason he hadn't joined a fraternity at Tulane: he didn't have the money.

"Thank you, Father, for the offer, but I'm sure I wouldn't be able to afford it."

"Not to worry, young man!" Father Paul responded. I only offer lessons to students who are willing to earn them, through hard work and dedication."

After that, Martin met Father Paul every week. The first meeting wasn't at all what Martin expected. He brought an old chess set and a tattered notebook to a study room at Loyola's library, but Father Paul had other ideas.

"Come on, let's go for a walk!" he suggested, not bothering to look back as he moved toward the nearest exit.

Martin was in reasonably good shape, thanks to his rugby club, but he had to push himself to keep up with the long-legged Jesuit as he led him on a forced march around the Garden District in New Orleans.

"So, tell me about yourself," Father Paul suggested.

Martin was a bit out of sorts, having expected a quiet hour of tutoring at the chess board. "Well, Father, I'm interested in history..."

"No, No!" Father Paul interrupted. "Start from the beginning. Let's say, where you were born."

For the next hour, Martin experienced the friendliest but most complete interrogation of his life. He had intended to provide a bare outline, but found himself answering penetrating questions driven by the Jesuit's boundless curiosity. By the time their conversation was over, Father Paul knew everything he wanted to know about Martin, and he liked what he saw.

"You've had the most interesting upbringing," Father Paul surmised. "Cuba, Lebanon, even more exotic places like Appalachia." Glancing over his shoulder, Father Paul was pleased to see Martin found the contrast just as amusing as he did.

"Have you used your languages much?" the Father asked in fluent French, not his native Cajun dialect.

"Yes, often enough," Martin responded in kind. "I've been working summers as an interpreter for the port authority."

"How's your Arabic?" Father Paul continued, using the language in question.

"Not as good as my French, but workable," Martin answered, making no attempt to hide his surprise. "Where did you, I mean how...?"

"In Palestine," Father Paul offered. "I lived in the Holy land for many years. We can talk about that some other day, if you like."

"I would like that, very much," Martin remarked, deeply impressed with his new tutor.

When their walk was over, Father Paul surprised Martin yet again. "Well, young man, you can forget about those chess lessons." Martin's heart sank, for a moment, until he heard the rest of what Father Paul had to say. "That would be a waste of time. I'll tutor you in languages, if you like. That's where your real talent lies, based on everything I've heard from your professors-- and seen for myself. What do you say to that?"

Martin, accepted, of course, and met Father Paul twice a week after that. The extra work was a burden at first, but encouraged by Father Paul, Martin switched majors from history to foreign languages and the over-lapping effort began to pay off. Although it wasn't al-ways obvious, Martin also received subtle lessons on how to move about effectively in other societies, not just by speaking a foreign language but by understanding its cultural context. That was a subject Martin learned as a child but had yet to experience as an adult.

Father Paul also expressed an interest in Martin's social life, including his relationship with Fatima. He handled the question delicately, with a sensitivity appreciated by Martin, during one of their long forced marches.

Most of all, Father Paul wanted to know if Martin understood why he fell in love with Fatima, and how he handled their parting. As a young man who was used to keeping his inner life to himself, it was a relief for Martin to have someone he could talk to, someone he could confide in.

During one such conversation with Father Paul, Martin described the first time he met Fatima.

It happened early in Fatima's freshman year. Classes were done for the day and a group of students were playing volleyball in a small field, enjoying one of those fine southern days that stretched slowly into fall. Martin noticed Fatima right away, and so did all the other young men. When the games were done and the crowd began to drift away, Fatima was approached by one of the most prominent upperclassmen, a trust-fund boy who offered to give the exotic young freshman a ride in his Porsche, a gift from a father with more money than time to spend on his son. Fatima politely turned him down and seemed to glance in Martin's direction as her would-be suitor drove away.

Much to his surprise, Fatima approached Martin as he sat in the shade of a huge magnolia, drinking a can of root beer as he rested his back against the trunk. Martin was even more surprised when Fatima sat down beside him, instead of waiting for Martin to stand up, as any southern girl would have done.

"Hello," she said, with a clear voice and a gentle smile. You're that unusual boy with a Lebanese mother, aren't you?"

Martin was speechless at first. He knew plenty of other girls at the university, but the attractive ones always seemed to be playing a game with rules he barely understood; they were the daughters of doctors, lawyers and prominent businessmen, well-trained by their mothers to make a good catch for themselves. If they weren't playing their mothers' game, they were playing a different one, acting out and rebelling against their parents' expectations. Since Martin was neither rich nor dangerous-looking, he didn't appear on the radar screen for the typical coed at a private school like Tulane. Fatima was different, and she didn't seem to mind when Martin took a few moments to answer.

"Yes," Martin responded, as he nodded his head. "And you're that strange girl with a Persian father." Martin glanced sideways at Fatima and smiled, to make sure she didn't take offense. But that wasn't necessary at all. Fatima erupted in laughter, and the sound of her voice, in Martin's parched ears, was a life-giving spring of cool, flowing water.

"I've wanted to meet you," Fatima admitted. "I feel a bit lost here at the University, and was hoping someone like yourself, I mean, someone with family in the Middle East, might help me feel a little less like a stranger in a strange land."

"So you've read Robert Heinlen?" Martin asked, hoping to avoid talking about his embarrassing family.

"I love science fiction," Fatima answered enthusiastically. "Not for the fantasy, that doesn't appeal to me at all. The really good stuff stretches my imagination, it sort of forces me to question my assumptions. Do you know what I mean? Sometimes I feel like I'm surrounded by people who think they've already got all the answers, and I'm the only one still trying to figure out the questions."

"Your father's a professor, isn't he?" Martin asked, with a slight mocking tone in his voice. "Did he teach you to talk like that?"

"Yes," Fatima responded. "But he's trying to teach me how to think, not what I should think. He has more respect for me than that."

Martin pulled himself back from his memories and returned to his conversation with Father Paul. "I'd never met anyone like her, Father," the younger man confessed. "She challenged me in every way, but left herself open, vulnerable, completely exposed. She hid nothing from me--and I found myself embracing ideas I'd always rejected."

"Like what?" Father Paul asked, never missing an opportunity to ask an open-ended question, a lifelong habit that was endearing to some but irritating to others.

"Like true love, and the possibility that a lonely soul can recognize its mate, with no special introductions needed." Martin looked up and held his head high, hoping the older man wouldn't dismiss his feelings as mere sentiment.

Father Paul nodded his head politely and encouraged Martin to finish his story. "So tell me, Martin," he asked. "What did the two of you do after that, the first time you met?"

"It was incredible!" Martin continued. "We felt like we were in a little world of our own, a quiet space and a thrilling place where we could abandon all pretense and simply exist, as ourselves, with no show, no acting. We had to keep moving, we couldn't keep still, so we took the trolley down to the French Quarter and over to Jackson Square. We walked and talked for hours, along the river bank, on the paddle boat over to the Zoo, until it was getting late and Fatima had to go home, so her father wouldn't worry. We held hands, the whole evening, Father, as if our lives depended on it. It was hard to say goodbye. The first time and the last time."

"You're very lucky, Martin," Father Paul remarked, as he stopped in the middle of the sidewalk. "Even if you never see Fatima again. The love you feel for her is real, as real as the God who made you. As we grow older, a man's heart can grow harder. I hope you'll find a way to remain open to love, both earthly and divine, even when it hurts." Having said all they had to say that day, the two men parted company.

Finally, in the middle of his senior year, Father Paul introduced Martin to his "friend," a recruiter who traveled all the way from the CIA's Headquarters in Virginia to conduct an interview. Some months later, in the fall of 1979, Martin was sworn in as a member of the Agency's Clandestine Service.

Chapter 23: A Dangerous Game

When Fatima reached her home in the Shahrak-e Gharb district in the northwestern quadrant of the city, she was relieved to find her husband away. She had nearly lost her nerve at Tehran International Airport, when a bored customs inspector opened her bag. Fortunately, a more senior officer spotted Fatima's diplomatic passport, which she acquired by virtue of her husband's privileged position, and waved her through with a respectful nod.

Fatima tossed her bag on a divan in her bedroom and opened it quickly. She found a package, which appeared to be a box containing a new telephone answering machine, and opened the box as instructed. Inside, she found an old-fashioned looking green telephone set, just like the one in her husband's study. How on earth, she wondered, had the Israelis managed to get their hands on one of the secret telephones used by the most senior Revolutionary Guards officials, those who needed to be able to conduct sensitive conversations at home? She remembered her husband bragging that the phones were scrambled, using dedicated land lines and an unbreakable code, and that only a few dozen top officers shared his privilege.

Despite his cruelty, Fatima sometimes felt sorry for her husband; born to a working-class family in a culture that glorified its intellectual and cultural elite, her husband was never content, always in search of her approval, while hating her for needing it.

Eager to find some relief from the pressure that haunted her, Fatima moved quickly to fulfill her task, before her husband came home from work. She walked into her husband's study, which was always unlocked, and replaced her husband's special phone with the identical one supplied by the Israelis.

The connection was simple and only took a moment. She had been warned not to throw the old phone out with the trash, because the item was rare and could easily be traced back to her husband. Instead, she carefully wrapped the phone in some brown paper and hid the package in a box of women's clothes, in a dusty corner of her attic. Now, with the most dangerous part of her task completed, Fatima tried to relax, to adjust to a role she hoped would only last for a few weeks.

Fatima's husband, however, would not be returning home any time soon. He was meeting with General Suleimani at Quds Force HQS, and the General was livid:

"Somehow, the Americans had been warned about our secret relationship with Al-Qaeda, and we must find the source of the leak," the General said. "The lives of every man in this room are at stake. Only five officers knew about the operation, and all five of us are here in this room. Everyone else believes the Arabs were simply allowed to transport a handful of Stinger missiles through our territory. That means one of you is the source of this leak. The only question is: do we have a traitor in our midst, or has someone betrayed the Revolution through an act of carelessness?"

Fatima's husband, Colonel Sattar Fakoor, stood at attention as the General walked among his subordinates, staring into their faces, looking for any sign of guilt. After a moment, the General returned to his desk and barked out his orders:

"All of you will return to your offices immediately. You will prepare a statement describing the dates, times and participants in every meeting where the secrets of this operation were discussed. Your statements must be complete and they must be submitted to me within 48 hours. Take care, for your statements will be checked and cross-referenced during the course of the investigation, which I will lead. I promise it will be a thorough one. Dismissed."

As his subordinates filed out of his office, the General turned to face the large window behind his desk and took a deep breath. He knew he was safe, because he had already met with President Mahmoud Ahmadinejad earlier that morning, and the President was not overly unduly concerned. Ahmadinejad had issued a few instructions to his staff, calling for the usual denials and counter-accusations regarding America's vain attempts to justify an attack on Iran. He also told the General to go ahead and implement plans to provide the location of Usama Bin Laden and his top lieutenants to the Americans, using a back channel with the U.S. Ambassador in Lebanon.

During the meeting at Ahmadinejad's office, the President had offered his assurances:

"Don't worry, General, if the Americans attack, we may suffer some pain, to be sure, but the Revolution will be secured for generations to come. With our help, the Shia will rise up and drive the remnants of America's forces from Iraq, so our friends can seize control of the government. In their anger and frustration, the Americans will be sure to strike Al-Qaeda and the Sunni devils twice as hard as they strike us. From the chaos, we will rise stronger than ever, God willing."

General Suleimani was honored to serve a man with such vision. He only had to prepare his organization for the war to come, to ensure it emerged with the resources needed to help protect the Revolution.

Chapter 24: Scapegoats

Several days had passed since the news broke regarding Iran's involvement in providing support to Al-Qaeda. In the interim, Russian intelligence had collected detailed information on initial American preparations for a massive military strike against Iran. In addition, the U.S. Ambassador had met with the Russian Foreign Minister in Moscow and insisted that the Government of Russia take immediate steps to determine if its weapons of mass destruction or related technologies were indeed being supplied to Al-Qaeda, with assistance from Iran.

Pacing back and forth in his office in Moscow, Prime Minister Putin immediately recognized the need to create a diversion, to deflect any blame that might be directed at Russia should the Al-Qaeda plot succeed. He saw no reason not to proceed, as planned, to protect Russia's vital national interests; after all, he believed the Americans should not be allowed to withdraw from Iraq and Afghanistan until they suffered a convincing defeat. Better yet, he hoped the Americans would entangle themselves in another war, this time with Iran.

If his plan succeeded, Putin knew the price of oil would reach new heights, after falling precipitously during the global recession. That would enable Russia to continue rebuilding its tattered military infrastructure, and American power would be overextended until it collapsed. From Putin's perspective, the fact that the Americans had uncovered the terrorist plot in advance was a minor inconvenience.

With renewed determination, Putin activated a contingency plan based on a model that worked well in the past; when faced with international condemnation for his brutal crackdown on Muslim separatists in Chechnya, Putin called on a special unit of the Federal Security Service, or FSB, to organize a deception. The FSB arranged a series of bombings at several apartment buildings in three Russian cities and successfully blamed the attacks on Chechen terrorists. The incident solidified internal Russian support for Putin's crackdown and deflected criticism from the West.

A new deception operation was implemented immediately. A small team of specially-trained FSB officers placed a tactical nuclear device, the same type of artillery round Al-Qaeda had been allowed to obtain, outside a Russian town in the foothills of the Caucasus mountains. A small Russian Army base and checkpoint for commercial trucking was located nearby. When the warhead went off, 2,000 men, women and children living in the town were killed instantly, along with more than 3000 soldiers. Shortly after the explosion, the unfortunate FSB team was liquidated by a special unit from Putin's personal security service and every shred of evidence was destroyed.

The Russian government's public response was ferocious. The Army launched a massive assault on remaining Chechen rebel bases in the Caucasus mountains and claimed the right of "hot pursuit" when some of the rebels crossed the mountainous border into the Republic of Georgia. The state-controlled media fanned the flames of Russian public opinion and large crowds in several major cities were allowed to lynch any unfortunate Chechen-looking men who happened to be out on the street.

A few hours after the explosion, fabricated claims of responsibility by a Chechen rebel faction were released. Representatives of Russian intelligence met with their American counterparts to provide the first in a series of fabricated reports describing how the Chechen mafia had succeeded in purchasing three of the tactical nuclear warheads: one of which was detonated when a truck bound for Moscow was stopped at the checkpoint, and two of which appeared to have disappeared inside Iran. The "corrupt Russian traitors" who sold the weapons were said to have been rounded up and shot, as an example to others. At the most senior levels, Russian officials assured their nervous American counterparts that special measures had been introduced to secure the rest of the country's nuclear arsenal; some of the officials suggested Russia would accept long-standing U.S. proposals for closer cooperation in this important area.

In public and in private, American officials expressed heartfelt sympathy for the Russian victims and their families. None of the intelligence reports and analysis prepared for the President and his senior advisors hinted at Russian culpability, beyond a failure to crack down on rampant corruption and bribery in the military. The reports cited other instances in which Russian military officers had sold weapons and explosives to Muslim extremists throughout Central Asia and the Caucasus, even when their own forces were at risk.

Although the long-term problem of Russian's inability to secure its arsenal was taken very seriously by U.S. policymakers, the short-term threat posed by the presence of at least two nuclear devices in the hands of Al-Qaeda was everyone's first concern, understandably so. A massive effort was launched to find and destroy the weapons before they could be used.

Chapter 25: Limited Options

President Obama's speech to the nation was televised around the world. Millions of people stopped what they were doing to listen, with a growing sense of alarm:

"My fellow Americans," the President began in a cool, confident fashion. "By now all of you have heard about the horrendous terrorist attack in Russia, carried out by Chechen separatists and close allies of Al-Qaeda. A few moments ago, I spoke with President Medvedyev and relayed the heartfelt condolences of the American people. I offered the government of Russia our hand in friendship and made it clear we will do everything in our power to help Russia find those responsible."

"We cannot leave Russia to stand alone because we are facing the same threat. Only by standing together can we defeat the terrorists and put weapons of mass destruction beyond their reach forever. Never has this cause been more urgent, for we face a grave threat to our nation."

"Ladies and gentlemen, with help from our allies around the world, we have learned that the Islamic Republic of Iran is involved in a conspiracy to allow Al-Qaeda to acquire weapons of mass destruction, very likely the same type of tactical nuclear weapons used during the attack inside Russia. Our experts believe Al-Qaeda plans to use these weapons in attacks on the U.S. and our forces in Iraq. This threat appears to be credible and I want to assure the American people your government is doing everything in its power to avert the kind of tragedy that struck our friends in Russia today."

Looking up from his prepared speech, the President spoke directly to the camera:

"To the leaders of Iran, I make the following demands, which must be met within the next 10 days: arrest and hand over any members of Al-Qaeda hiding in your country. If weapons of mass destruction are passing through your territory, seize those weapons immediately and return them to the Government of Russia. In addition, Iran must arrest and detain any members of its Government involved in this plot and deliver them to the International Criminal Court, so they can stand trial for their crimes against humanity. Failure to comply with our demands will have immediate and dire consequences. Let me make this clear: the Government of the United States of America reserves the right to use any means at its disposal to compel a satisfactory response to our just and reasonable demands."

The President spoke from the Oval Office, so there was no opportunity for the press to ask questions. Instead, talking heads sparred on every channel, with many conservatives calling for an immediate strike on Iran and some liberals suggesting that the intelligence had been cooked up by the far right to justify the invasion of Iran they had been unable to muster before the end of the Bush administration. Ordinary Americans were simply angry, confused and fearful.

Immediately after his speech, President Obama held a private meeting with two of his closest advisors, just minutes before a larger meeting with his entire cabinet.

"Let's start with you, Rahm," the President said as he turned to his Chief of Staff.

"You're going to hear a full range of options during the cabinet meeting, Mr. President," Mr. Emmanuel responded. "Some are calling for a preemptive response, an immediate but limited strike on Iran's intelligence and security apparatus, a sample of what we could do if the Iranian government rejects our demands. Others are taking a wait-and-see attitude. Even with the bombing inside Russia, we don't know if the intelligence on Iranian cooperation with Al-Qaeda is true. Most of the experts find the story hard to believe."

"Right. What about you, Joe," the President said, turning to Vice President Biden.

"I'd rule out a preemptive response, Mr. President," the Vice President responded. "What would be the point of bombing Iran now? That won't stop an Al-Qaeda attack that's already in the works. I think we should push as hard as we can on the diplomatic front, with the goal of convincing the Iranian government it's in their interest to cooperate. If we confirm some Iranians are involved, we can choose the most appropriate response at that time."

"I agree, Joe. Our first priority is to stop an attack on the homeland, before it happens. We should point everything we have in that direction. If there is an attack, and the Iranians are really involved, we'll have no choice but to retaliate."

President Obama politely dismissed the Vice President and his Chief of Staff, so he could have a few moments alone to gather his thoughts.

After the cabinet meeting, Presidential orders needed to stop the expected terrorist attacks went into effect. National Guard and regular Army troops were deployed along the border with Mexico and Canada. All vehicular traffic into the country was stopped. Thousands of people abandoned their cars and trucks in hopes of gaining entry to the United States on foot. Within hours, the crowds became unruly and riots broke out at the largest border crossings in Texas and California. Since the tactical warhead used in the attack in Russia was relatively small and could be concealed in air freight, all incoming flights were cancelled and aircraft were diverted or returned to their point of origin. In addition, every ship headed for American ports was ordered to stop outside U.S. waters.

When the President's order was issued, a Liberian registered freighter--the Commercial Atlantic--was well out to sea, having unloaded its lethal cargo in the U.S. two days beforehand.

The markets opened in Asia a few hours after the President's speech. Already low, stock prices plummeted ever further and the price of oil skyrocketed to over $200 a barrel, with no end in sight. Gold and other precious metals soared in value as panicky investors rushed to find a refuge for the money they hadn't already lost. Despite the best efforts of the Obama administration, the fragile American economy slipped over the edge and the carnage on Wall Street was worse than the sell-off in late 2008 and early 2009.

It was hard to believe, at the time, but things were going to get worse, far worse, before they got better.

Chapter 26: Terrorism and Democracy

The morning after the President's speech on Iran and the threat of nuclear terrorism, Dr. Samantha Jones, a Professor of political science at the University of Wisconsin in Madison, was interviewed by National Public Radio personality Nora Daily in a nationwide broadcast. Dr. Jones, a brilliant African-American academic who grew up in Oakland and studied at Stanford University, was promoting her new book, "Terrorism and Democracy: Assessing the Threat."

"So, Dr. Jones, your new book is timely indeed. What do you make of the President's speech?" Daily asked.

"I believe the President has every right to fulfill his responsibilities as Commander in Chief, assuming the information on Iranian involvement is accurate." Dr. Jones campaigned for Barack Obama during the election in the fall of 2008, but she valued her intellectual objectivity and didn't want to be dismissed as a partisan supporter of a Democratic president. She was also deeply concerned about the current crisis and hoped the country wouldn't be drawn into another debilitating war.

"Of course, Dr. Jones. But let's talk about the central premise of your book, your argument that terrorism doesn't represent a threat to the American way of life."

"That's true, Nora. I don't believe terrorists can destroy our way of life, unless we do their work for them."

"But what do you mean, Professor? Didn't they kill more than 3,000 Americans on 9/11?"

"That's true, Nora, and a reprehensible act it was. What's missing is a sense of perspective. Far more Americans are killed every year by drugs, drunk drivers and handguns than by terrorists, yet no one is arguing we should made fundamental changes in our society to address those problems."

"I'm not sure if I see the connection, Professor. May I call you Samantha?"

"Yes, of course, Nora. Please let me explain. The Bush administration argued that our country needed to make fundamental changes in the rule of law--the Patriot Act, for example--in order to address the threat posed by terrorism. The threat was so dire, according to this line of thinking, we needed to suspend the constitution."

"Please go on," Nora encouraged.

"Thank you," the Professor responded, as she took a quick sip of water. "Any objective study shows terrorism is, in fact, no threat to our way of life whatsoever. Yes, terrorists can kill some Americans, perhaps many Americans, but terrorism cannot destroy our Constitution, our Republic, our armed forces or even our economy, unless we overreact. The only hope the terrorists have, when using asymmetrical warfare, is to force us to overreact, to do their work for them."

"I'm not sure if I understand what you mean by 'doing their work for them.' Would you elaborate?" Nora asked.

"I'll try. Take a look at Palestinian terrorists, for example. When they attack Israel, they're trying to kill Israeli citizens, it's true, but more than that, they're trying to provoke the Israeli government into overreacting. For example, every time the Israeli Army accidently kills a

139

Palestinian civilian, in an understandable effort to destroy a Palestinian terrorist who attacked them, the terrorists win more support from the Muslim world. At the same time, any Palestinian who might otherwise support a peaceful solution is marginalized."

"I know it's hard for us to understand, but the terrorists actually win whenever Israel kills a Palestinian, innocent or not, so the terrorists want to provoke the Israeli government into killing, or arresting and detaining, as many of their fellow Palestinians as possible. We saw the same thing happen in Iraq and Afghanistan. It's sick and twisted, I know, but it's been an effective strategy, from the terrorists' point of view."

"I think I see what you mean, Samantha, but shouldn't our government do everything it can to protect our citizens? Isn't national defense the government's highest responsibility?"

"Yes, that's true, and you're getting right to the heart of the matter. As the saying goes, the devil is in the details. The question is, what exactly do we mean when we declare the government should do 'everything' it can? Do the majority of Americans believe 'everything' should include the use of torture or the suspension of our constitutional rights? I think not."

"Let's take an analogy," the Professor continued. "We used to talk about the War on Drugs, and everyone is concerned about drug-related violence in our inner cities. Does that mean the government should do 'everything' it can to fight the problem? For example, should the government evacuate our inner cities, demolish the slums and forcibly distribute poor minorities in small towns throughout the country, in an attempt to solve our nation's problems with drugs, guns, gangs, poor schools and the hereditary cycle of poverty? Should we suspend the writ of habeas corpus, use torture to extract confessions from known drug dealers and conduct wiretaps without judicial warrant? Of course not. Everyone agrees that would be illegal and immoral."

"I see where you're going with this, Samantha, but people are scared. What about the threat of nuclear terrorism? You saw what just happened in Russia. Doesn't that represent a real and present danger to our way of life?"

"That's almost unthinkable, Nora, isn't it? I believe the loss of even one life to terrorism is a tragedy, much less the loss of thousands of innocent men, women and children. Of course we would want our government to stop such an attack before it happens, if at all possible."

"Still, for the sake of argument, let's consider the implications; any objective expert on physical security will tell you it's impossible to make an open society like ours completely secure. By objective expert, I mean someone who hasn't profited from the billions of dollars worth of Pentagon and Homeland Security contracts after 9/11."

"Our economy, our prosperity, our very way of life, requires relatively open borders to sustain itself. We could spend 100 or 1,000 times as much on physical security and that still wouldn't make our airlines, our ports or our cities completely safe from terrorism. Take a look around, even notorious dictatorships and police states have experienced terrorism."

"So, what do you think we should do, Dr. Jones? Simply look the other way and allow terrorist attacks to happen?"

"Of course not, Nora, but this brings up a fundamental question that arises whenever we address a serious problem in a civil society. There are many things we could do, as a nation, in response to a given threat, but what should we do?"

"This question leads to other questions: how do we respond to terrorism in an effective manner, while protecting the rule of law, the very thing that separates us from our enemies? Is it possible that a futile attempt to make ourselves perfectly safe could cause more damage to our way of life than any terrorist attack ever could? Is it possible we could unleash unintended consequences, perhaps more dangerous than the terrorists we face today, if we tried to use preemptive military force against every potential threat we face in the world?"

The Professor continued: "In a misguided effort to achieve perfect physical security, which isn't attainable in the first place, at what point would we become a non-democracy, a country no longer capable of inspiring others to emulate us?"

"Believe me, Nora, I'm no pacifist. My father served in the Navy during WWII and my older brother died in Vietnam. I honor their memories and wish our soldiers success as they try to fulfill their difficult missions in Iraq and Afghanistan."

"At the same time, I believe we should make an effort to develop a sense of perspective, based on careful reason and analysis, before we throw out the constitutional protections that have served us so well. As far as I'm concerned, any threat incapable of destroying our way of life is insufficient reason to dismantle our way of life ourselves."

"But what about the underlying causes of terrorism, Samantha? A large portion of your book deals with this issue."

"Yes, of course, Nora. The root causes of terrorism are complex and I imagine we won't have time to get into that in any detail during this program. But I would like to say the first step in developing a more reasonable response to terrorism is to accept the fact that there are indeed causes we can identify and understand. If we take that step, we might be surprised to discover there are things we can do to make it harder for organizations like Al-Qaeda to recruit new terrorists, while dealing with existing terrorists in a forceful manner."

"Here again," the professor continued, "I believe there's a useful analogy, when you examine our domestic problems. For example, we can arrest and imprison as many young men of color as we want, but we'll never eliminate crime in our inner cities until we address the underlying causes. Yes, we can and should hold adults accountable for the crimes they commit, but we also have to hold society responsible by at least making an attempt to identify and eliminate the root causes."

"To illustrate this point, how can a two-year-old boy be responsible for the circumstances he's born into if his mother is a crack addict and his father is a convict? We can blame it all on his parents, and just say its a 'black problem,' but that's not going to stop that little boy from becoming a gangster when he grows up. We can stick our heads in the sand and pretend there's no reason why that boy shouldn't be able to pull himself up by his own bootstraps, while ignoring the fact that the odds are stacked against him."

143

"In the same way, we can capture, torture and kill as many terrorists as we want, but that won't make it any harder for organizations like Al-Qaeda to recruit all the replacements they need. Yes, we can blame it on the Arabs, or simply say it's a 'Muslim problem,' but we're never going to eliminate terrorism until we at least consider the possibility that we can resolve some of the root causes. One of the motivations that drove me to write this book was a firm conviction that we need to begin a national dialogue on this very subject."

"In your book, Samantha, you say the War on Terrorism can't be won. As a result, some of your critics have labeled you a defeatist. What did you mean by that statement?"

"I've taken a bit of heat for that remark but I stand by my position. The explanation is simple, really. We can't win a War on Terrorism because terrorism is a tactic, not a nation or a government we can defeat. Terrorism has been used throughout history, both by small groups that could not otherwise challenge a greater power, or even by great nations that wanted to enhance their traditional military power."

"Let me cite a specific example: although most Americans agree the Second World War was a just war, the fire bombing of thousands of civilians in Germany, not to mention the dropping of nuclear bombs on two Japanese cities, was a deliberate effort to sow terror and a sense of inevitable defeat in the enemy's civilian population. The goal of saving American lives and shortening the war was honorable, from our perspective, but the end result, from the perspective of the innocent women and children on the ground in Germany and Japan, was no different than the terror experienced by the innocent victims of 9/11."

"That is a controversial position, Dr. Jones. Are you saying Americans are terrorists, too?"

"Not at all, Nora. I'm simply drawing attention to the fact that terrorism, per se, can't be defeated because it's a tactic that anyone or any group could use in a military conflict. By bundling the Wars in Iraq and Afghanistan together into an overarching 'War on Terrorism,' the Bush administration made it much more difficult for the country to engage in a rational discussion. We need to do that before we can begin to develop policies that might actually enable us to resolve the underlying causes of Islamic terrorism."

"You're obviously not the first expert to make this suggestion, Dr. Jones, but what exactly do you see as the underlying causes of terrorism?"

"Well, Nora, this is an area where the Bush Administration was partially right. The absence of freedom and democracy in the Muslim world is indeed one of the key underlying causes of terrorism. Where the Bush administration fell short, in my opinion, was in the substance of its foreign policy."

"Can you be more specific, Dr. Jones?"

"Certainly. I believe part of the problem is an absence of understanding that is very basic in our society. American democracy is so robust and so self-sustaining, many of our fellow Americans have a very superficial impression when it comes to understanding how our democracy works."

"For example, my department conducted a nationwide poll, and the results show the majority of

145

Americans believe free markets and fair elections are the only thing needed to establish a new democracy. Many in the same group believe the U.S. did everything it could to help the Iraqis and Afghanis establish democracy for themselves, simply by removing Saddam Hussein and the Taliban and setting up new elections. As a result, many Americans blame the Iraqis and the Afghanis for failing to take advantage of the opportunity we gave them."

"What reasons would you give for our apparently failed experiments in nation building?" Nora asked.

"I'll try to explain," Dr. Jones responded confidently. "As it turns out, the facts on the ground show the establishment of democracy is much more complex than the Bush administration imagined. Elections are an important part of the process, but only one part. All three branches of government--the executive, the legislative and the the judicial--have to earn the trust of a majority of citizens before a stable government can be established. A sufficient number of Iraqis and Afghanis have to place their loyalty to a unified country above the interests of their tribe, their ethnic group and their religious sect, and we're still not sure if that will happen. In fact, a sufficient number of Iraqis and Afghanis must be willing to fight and die for a united, democratic country before those goals can be achieved, no matter how successful the surges may have been and no matter what the United States does in the future."

"I understand your point, Samantha, but what does all that have to do with the underlying causes of terrorism?"

"Let me try to explain, Nora, by making an analogy that should make sense to our fellow Americans.

146

First, let's start by looking back at the American Revolution. We fought against taxation without representation, to free ourselves from domination by a distant British monarch. The British authorities were heavy-handed at times and didn't always show respect for the colonists. Otherwise, life in colonial America wasn't too shabby, except of course for the slaves."

"Now, let's take a look at the conditions under which the typical citizen of Saudi Arabia, Egypt or just about any other Arab nation lives today. I think it would be fair to say the typical Arab has a hundred times more reason to overthrow his own government than we had to overthrow the British back in 1776."

"Don't get me wrong, I'm grateful for our founding fathers and the Constitution they created, but I believe we Americans would be much closer to understanding the underlying causes of Islamic terrorism if we could develop a better appreciation for our own history. If we can understand why the American colonists were willing to separate themselves from Great Britain, through the force of arms, we should be able to understand why many Muslims are willing to use force to bring about much-needed change in their own countries."

"So what are you saying, Dr. Jones? That just about every Arab country in the world needs a revolution?" The veteran NPR correspondent glanced at the clock on the wall behind Dr. Jones as her producer pointed at his watch.

"Yes, exactly that. A peaceful revolution, if at all possible, but who are we to forbid the Arab people from using force when we ourselves used force to gain our own freedom? Many Arabs have been struggling for decades to overthrow their despotic regimes, but with

147

little success. In fact, we've observed a heated debate between those extremists who believe their groups should focus on the elimination of their own nation's particular despot, and those extremists like Usama Bin Laden who argue the local despots will be easy to overthrow, once external sources of support have been eliminated."

"What do you mean by 'external support,' Dr Jones?"

"That would be the United States and the rest of the industrialized world, including Europe. Rightly or wrongly, many Muslims blame us for propping up dictators they believe they could otherwise eliminate without our interference."

"So you're saying Muslim revolutionaries blame us for all their problems? Do you think that's reasonable? If the extremists believe they're struggling for their freedom, why don't they stand up and fight, instead of resorting to terrorism and hiding behind their own civilian populations?"

"Let's tackle your last question first, Nora," Dr. Jones responded. "The reason Islamic extremists won't risk a conventional military conflict is simple: it wouldn't work. The extremists would be slaughtered by our overwhelming firepower, or the overwhelming power of their own governments, using weapons and training provided by the West. That may not seem 'fair,' but it doesn't change the reality on the ground."

"That brings up another area where the domestic political debate has been muddled. Strictly speaking, we shouldn't use the word terrorism to describe an attack on our military forces. That's combat. In fact, I believe we should be cautious when we use the word 'terrorism' to describe the killing of innocent bystanders when a roadside bomb is used to attack one of our military convoys. Otherwise, we open ourselves up to accusations of hypocrisy when our own military operations cause civilian casualties, which they often do. If we want the rest of the world to take us seriously, we need to reserve the word 'terrorism' to describe deliberate attacks on innocent civilians."

"Now let's tackle the question of blame, Nora. It doesn't matter what we think; it matters what the Muslim world thinks, if we want to minimize terrorism. When you consider the fact that the U.S. gives the Egyptian Government--a government ruled by an unelected and repressive dictatorship--billions of dollars every year, we can begin to understand why so many Muslims dismiss our foreign policy as hypocritical. They believe the U.S. is only concerned about removing dictators who represent a threat to our economic interests. They also believe other despots get a free pass and a hand up from the U.S. Government. That's one of the reasons why so many Muslims hate us and that's one of the reasons why a small percentage of Muslims are using terrorism as a tactic, in the hope of driving us out of their region so they can remove the despots themselves."

"But what about Saddam, Dr. Jones. If the Iraqi people were so eager to remove him, why didn't they take care of him on their own? Why did we have to do the job for them?"

"That's an excellent question, Nora, and I've made an effort to address that question in my book. In summary, Saddam was a particularly vicious and effective dictator who created a system that enabled him to hang on to power much longer than one might have expected. The Soviet Union was equally adept at suppressing internal dissent, but systemic flaws inherent to communism eventually caused the USSR to collapse, thankfully without the need for military conflict. I believe the same thing would have happened in Iraq, eventually."

"Well, if I understand what you're saying, then why don't we just wait for all those despotic regimes in the Muslim world to collapse on their own accord?" Nora asked.

"If we were neutral players," Dr. Jones responded, "we might be able to do that. But one fact that is missing in the debate here in the United States is the extent to which we are indeed responsible for propping up some of the most oppressive governments in the world. Egypt and Saudi Arabia are two of the best examples, but they aren't the only ones."

"The situation is really very tragic," the Professor continued. "Even if the Islamic extremists succeeded in removing one of the most repressive regimes in the region, any new Islamic government they establish would be no more capable of meeting the needs of the Arab people today than the old communist parties were able to meet the needs of Russia or Eastern Europe. Both models for organizing a society are failures and offer no viable solutions for the problems that plague the modern world. Still, who are we to dictate the form of government other people chose for themselves, if we can imagine having peaceful relations with such a government?"

"Now, a hard-headed realist might argue our friendly relations with countries like Saudi Arabia and Egypt are in our national interest. To be honest, a purely pragmatic approach to foreign policy would be perfectly legitimate if it were open, honest and consistent. As it now stands, our democracy agenda has no credibility whatsoever in the Muslim world when we only eliminate unfriendly tyrants, like Saddam, while coddling 'friendly' despots, like the Saudis and Egyptians."

"Of course, we could maintain our current hypocritical policies, in a naive or cynical fashion, but we would have to accept the consequences, which include more terrorism."

Genuinely puzzled, the NPR correspondent asked, "What other choice do we have? Should we simply allow radical jihadists to take over the Muslim world? Wouldn't they build new terrorist training camps and use them to launch attacks against us?"

"In some ways, it may be too late," Dr. Jones responded. "Our foreign policy has already caused grave damage. Does that mean we should retain the same failed policies? Would that make things better or worse?"

"Let me ask you and your listeners, Nora, to consider some alternatives, to gain a fresh perspective on the history of our relationship with the Muslim world, so we can look for the most productive way forward."

With great passion and conviction, Dr. Jones tried to drive home her point:

"What would have happened if we had stepped aside, years ago, and allowed events to take their course? For example, what if we hadn't replaced an elected government in Iran with the Shah, all those years ago? Would we face the same problems in our relationship with Iran today? What if the U.S. had insisted that

151

the military regime in Algeria accept the results of their election several years ago? Would there be so many Algerians involved in terrorism? What if we stopped propping up the Egyptian government? Would Al-Qaeda have been able to recruit so many Egyptian terrorists, or would the Egyptians turn their rage against their own government, the real source of their frustration? And finally, what if we stopped standing between the Arab people and the tyrants who rule them, simply to protect our short-term economic interests? Would we remain the focus of their anger?"

"I regret we've run out of time, Dr. Jones. I'm sure your controversial new book will generate a great deal of discussion over the next few weeks."

"My pleasure, Nora."

Chapter 27: A Target of Opportunity

When the ordinary-looking container from the Commercial Atlantic arrived at its final destination in Macon, Georgia, the bill of lading was signed by a French citizen named Jacques Pitard. The son of a failed French artist, Jacques was raised by his Algerian mother in a Muslim slum outside Paris after his father died of a drug overdose. Although Jacques adopted the nom de guerre Ismail when he studied the Koran with a group of young radicals, he kept the European name on his passport and the French features he inherited from his father.

A gifted mathematician, Jacques performed well during his state comprehensive examinations and earned a place in an electrical engineering program at a lesser French university. During his college years, Jacques spent his summers exploring the Muslim world, traveling on his French passport. He was eventually spotted and recruited by members of an Algerian terrorist group hiding in Pakistan. Although he volunteered to join other foreign fighters immediately after the American invasion of Iraq, Jacques was destined for greater things.

Much to his mother's pleasure, Jacques accepted a junior position with a French electrical engineering firm in a quiet town near the Swiss border. He appeared to abandon his radical Muslim friends and seemed to live a secular life. He continued to travel, ostensibly to pursue his interest in photography.

Jacques never told anyone about his subsequent trips to Pakistan, which were conducted in alias using a false passport provided by the brothers in Marseilles. He relished the training he obtained at several camps in the mountains of Waziristan--particularly the chance to work with explosives. Eventually, given his technical education and other unique qualifications, Jacques was selected for a very important mission. During a trip to Canada a year after his training was completed, Jacques slipped across the border to America.

Jacques was assisted by Philippe Broussard, a young French-Canadian from Montreal who inherited an intense hatred of America from his mother, a well-known activist from Quebec. A devoted Marxist for much of her life, Philippe's mother converted to Islam when she lost her faith in the Communist party as the Warsaw pact began to crumble in the late 1980s.

That was a few years after she met Philippe's father, an Algerian refugee who embraced the forgotten Islam of his fathers when it became clear the Communist revolution he hoped for was not going to free his native land from the tyrannical military regime he despised. Six members of his immediate family had been murdered by that regime and he was determined to avenge their deaths, in any way possible.

Philippe's parents never married, but his mother drew strength from her new religion and raised her son to be a devout Muslim, with help from a conservative mosque funded by the Government of Saudi Arabia. When he graduated from high school, the mosque provided financial support so Philippe could perform the sacred pilgrimage, the Hajj, to Mecca. During the trip, Philippe was discovered by a supporter of of Al-Qaeda who ran a guest house for foreign pilgrims. Young men like Philippe, who looked and acted like ordinary North Americans with a European heritage, were in great demand.

"Jacques," Philippe asked his older partner, "how can we possibly do it? You saw the news this morning. All the roads leading to Washington and Manhattan are closed and every vehicle is being searched. We have to select another target!"

Jacques knew his young friend was right, but he was reluctant to change their plans. For the third time in as many hours, he tried to think of some ruse that would enable them to proceed with one of their primary targets. So much trust had been put in him, how could he disappoint his brothers or the sheik? Finally, Jacques came up with an inspiration, an idea he had suggested himself when he was first briefed on the operation.

"Philippe," Jacques asked, "Have you ever been to Orlando?" At first, the young Canadian simply stared at Jacques, his eyes blinking rapidly as he considered the implications. Suddenly, the idea sunk in, and Philippe laughed out loud as he embraced the older Frenchman enthusiastically.

"That's fantastic!" Philippe shouted. "We're going to Disney World!" he shouted, mocking the irritating TV commercial he'd seen so many times.

The two men threw their last remaining personal items in the back of a white rental van and hit the road. By the time they reached Orlando, it was almost midnight. Philippe was exhausted and fell asleep immediately in their cheap hotel room. Jacques was restless and sat up in bed, smoking and ruminating for a couple of hours. When he woke in the morning, Philippe was already up, showered and dressed.

"Jacques, we have to see it first; as tourists, I mean. We can do it tomorrow--the place will be packed on a

155

Saturday. But first we have to take a look around, you know, so we can case the place."

Jacques looked at his young friend and nodded.

"You're right, tomorrow would be better. First, let's say our prayers, and then we'll play tourist."

The two men prayed solemnly toward Mecca and rose quietly from their meditations. When they emerged from their motel room, they were greeted by a blinding sun. It was a perfect spring morning and several children were playing in the parking lot, thrilled by their upcoming adventure.

The traffic was heavy as Jacques and Philippe made the short drive to Disney World. Finally, after what seemed like an eternity, they parked their van in the middle of a huge parking lot and walked over to a bus stop. When the shuttle bus reached its destination, Jacques saw a large crowd waiting at the main entrance. There appeared to be extra security at the gates and every bag was being carefully searched.

At that moment, Jacques realized there was no reason to delay. This was no ordinary truck bombing and they didn't need to get any closer to the target than the parking lot, where the Sword of the Prophet waited.

Jacques grabbed the young Canadian by the arm and looked him square in the face. He realized Philippe was too young to accept responsibility for what had to be done. He would have to take everything on himself.

"Philippe, I can't go with you today. There's no need to case this place. We'll just come back tomorrow morning, as you suggested. For my part, I need to make some technical preparations, to make sure everything goes the way it should, God willing. Why don't you go

156

ahead and enjoy yourself? Play the tourist, look at the young women, for tomorrow you'll receive your reward in paradise."

Philippe argued with the older man for a few minutes, to save face. The last time Jacques saw Philippe, he was smiling and waving as he worked his way through the crowds.

Jacques was filled with icy determination. How could the Americans enjoy such frivolity, when millions of Muslims were suffering under repressive regimes, exploited by their own governments, with help from a handful of rich countries? The Americans had the most to answer for, he believed. They were responsible for arming Israel to the point where any direct attack by the surrounding Muslim nations was bound to fail. The Americans looked the other way when the Israelis developed nuclear weapons, when the Palestinians were driven from their homes, when tens of thousands of innocent men and women were killed during the wars in Iraq and Afghanistan. Most of all, the Americans remained silent when the murderous regime in Algeria overthrew a legitimate election, preventing his father's people from establishing the Islamic republic they desired.

No, there was only one solution. If the Americans refused to open their eyes to the suffering around them, he would have to open them himself, Insh'allah.

Twenty minutes later, Philippe and more than 15,000 other men, women and children visiting Disney World were killed instantly when Jacques detonated the Sword of Allah. Thousands more were fatally wounded and many tens of thousands were injured by the blast and its aftermath.

The fires spread wildly, especially in the surrounding resorts. The early morning crowds at Epcot Center were knocked off their feet by the shock wave. Many of them caught a brief glimpse of a billowing mushroom cloud before the darkness fell, enveloping them in a storm of choking dust and debris. Faceless screams pierced the darkness and quieter voices were heard praying for salvation.

On the far side of the World, U.S. military commanders in Baghdad were trying to decide how they could possibly protect the new American Embassy-- much less the entire Green Zone--from a truck bomb attack using a tactical nuclear device. There was no answer in the playbook, because no one had seriously considered the threat.

Some of the officers said the area around the Embassy was impossible to defend, and that it would be best to evacuate civilian personnel and to disperse the troops and command structure to minimize casualties. The Ambassador rejected the idea and demanded the Army set up an outer perimeter at a suitable distance from the Green Zone, to protect the Embassy, civilians and military commands located in the heart of the zone.

At that point, the Army colonel whose troops would be responsible for carrying out such an order lost his cool:

"Are you out of your mind? I won't sacrifice my troops so you can hunker safely in your bunker. We have to disperse and we need to do so immediately. Haven't you noticed? Most of our Iraqi allies have already fled the zone and any civilian with a car or two feet is moving away from the area as fast as he can."

Just as the Ambassador rose to put the impudent colonel in his place, a young Army major ran into the room and reported to the General:

"Sir, it's already happening, the cable news channels are reporting a massive explosion at Disney World, in Orlando. They think it's a tactical nuke."

"Shit," the General said, just before he was blown across the room by a shock wave unlike anything he had experienced in his long and distinguished career.

Minutes after the nuclear attacks on Disney World and the Green Zone, small teams of terrorists were already in position at three separate locations around the country: JFK airport outside New York City; Reagan National Airport in northern Virginia; and Los Angeles International Airport. Each team included a missile operator, a driver and a spotter.

The missiles were provided by an ethnic Pushtun warlord from Afghanistan, a man with close ties to the Taliban. Although the Stingers were well past their designated shelf life, Usama Bin Laden had insisted on using the missiles because they were given to the mujahidin by the CIA during the Great Jihad against the Soviet Red Army. Divine justice, he thought.

The attack at Reagan National Airport was the easiest to execute. The terrorist team, already in place before the U.S. Government received reports of an imminent attack, positioned itself in a small riverside park at the end of the main runway. The spotter was responsible for selecting the largest possible aircraft, with the heaviest possible passenger and fuel load, within a certain time window. In this case, he selected a flight to

Denver, based on a bit of internet research that revealed the type of aircraft and the number of seats booked.

The spotter identified the target aircraft as soon as it positioned itself at the far end of the runway, ready for takeoff. While the missile operator emerged from a rented van and spun up the Stinger, the driver and spotter provided security. Two off-duty Marines in shorts and t-shirts, only months back from a tour of duty in Iraq, tried to charge the missile operator but were quickly gunned down. The crowd at the riverside park--mostly parents with young children who enjoyed watching the takeoffs and landings--scattered as best they could, some seeking refuge behind a stone jetty.

When the flight to Denver reached the end of the runway, it climbed quickly to the west, following the Potomac River toward the Pentagon, Arlington Cemetery and Memorial Bridge. With the engines burning at full throttle, the jet was an easy target for the Stinger's infrared seeker. The impact and explosion blew the right engine completely off the wing. The pilots struggled to retain control but the situation became hopeless when the right wing collapsed, causing the airliner to tumble into a north Arlington neighborhood less than three miles from the CIA's Headquarters complex in Langley, Virginia.

Minutes later, all three terrorists were shot and killed as they tried to execute a follow-up suicide attack on the airport's main terminal building.

Planned attacks at JFK airport in New York and Los Angeles International were unsuccessful. In New York, the team was stopped by police before they could deploy at a suitable location with line of sight on departing aircraft. The ensuing gun battle was brief but violent and ended when the last surviving terrorist was shot in the head by a sniper. In Los Angeles, the aging Stinger missile malfunctioned, much to the frustration of the terrorists. Determined to achieve martyrdom, the group executed a follow-up attack on the main terminal building. Due to quick reaction by the airport police, the terrorists were gunned down minutes after they tried to gain access. Although several innocent bystanders were killed and dozens were wounded, it could have been worse, far worse.

With no way of knowing how many terrorists might still be in the country, all civilian airports were closed until the threat could be evaluated and additional security resources deployed. Tens of thousands of passengers were stranded and air freight services ground to a halt, further straining an economy and an air transport system already disrupted by the cancellation of incoming international flights.

Chapter 28: Resurrection Island

Boris Nikolayevich Mystikov sat in the jump seat of a Kazakh Army helicopter as it flew west toward Resurrection Island, where the dying Aral Sea used to be. Boris was on the run, but he wasn't planning to run very far.

Boris was in Almaty, the former capital of Kazakhstan and still its largest city, when he received a telephone call and a sharp warning from an old friend in Moscow. He and every other participant in the plot to sell weapons of mass destruction to Iran and Al-Qaeda were to be rounded up and shot.

Boris had been in Moscow just days before, celebrating the most successful mission of his career, an operation that would cause more damage to Russia's main enemy--the United States--than any other effort in the history of Russian intelligence. It was only by chance that he found himself out of the country when the order came down to shoot the same people who had served the nation so well.

Boris, for one, was not going to be slaughtered like a dog by some stranger. He would take matters into his own hands.

The Russian was in no mood to chat with his pilots, young men who believed they were escorting a VIP on a short trip to view the remains of a deserted Soviet military base. Boris had numerous connections in the Kazakh government and found it easy to pull a few strings, ostensibly to arrange a quick day trip that might yield a valuable business opportunity.

Boris sat quietly, staring out across the vast wasteland of a dead and dying sea. The sea floor, now a barren desert, was streaked with black and white, as if a tribe of giants had amused themselves by tossing huge bags of charcoal and flour over the horizon, only to watch in laughter as the bags exploded when they hit the ground.

Dust devils danced where fishermen once cast their nets. The endless sky was filthy, like the heavens over Los Angeles on a hot summer's day. Boris' body remembered the past better than his mind; he had to suppress an overwhelming urge to strip and shower, to wash away the dust and dirt that seemed to settle in every pore and crevice, when the desert winds blew.

As his eyes scanned the horizon, Boris saw something, a large, dark shape that caught his eye. There! And there again! Several large ships, two freighters and at least one patrol boat lay on their sides in the desert-- silent, rusting hulks with no sea to support them and no ports to welcome them.

Moments later, the former island--now a large plateau--rose into view. Stark cliffs circled the ruins of an abandoned city, with apartment blocks, office buildings, schools, a small airport, laboratories, barracks, even a cinema.

The dust rose in a swirling cloud as the helicopter landed in the abandoned town square. Wasting no time, Boris headed straight for the door and jumped down immediately.

"Be careful, sir, a pack of wolves was spotted in the area last week!" The pilot felt responsible for the older man's safety.

"Don't worry, captain, I'll be back in an hour. If the wolves catch me, you can leave my bones in the desert!"

The young pilots laughed as Boris ducked, holding on to his hat as he walked across the square. With a stiff breeze blowing across the desert, a cloud of dust surrounding the helicopter swirled as the turbines were disengaged, enveloping an abandoned theater in a brief sand storm.

Not sure if his will would last, Boris walked due north to the largest of three office buildings on the square. As he passed through the main entrance, no longer guarded or enclosed by glass, Boris imagined he heard his former lover--a gifted doctor and medical researcher assigned to the base--greeting him with the bright voice of her younger days. Boris felt a punch in his stomach when her voice was replaced by an image that had haunted him for 20 years: Marina's lifeless body in the hospital morgue, raped and murdered by two drunken soldiers from Dushanbe.

Boris still felt responsible for Marina's death, for the fight he started earlier that evening. They were sitting at a private table in the base officer's club when it began.

For months, Marina had pleaded with Boris not to extend his tour of duty on the island. She wanted to move on, to conduct medical research, to heal the sick. Until that night, she'd never explained why. He replayed the conversation in his mind:

"I've got some good news!" Boris began, with the intention of putting his woman in her place, her dreams and desires subordinate to his own. "I've agreed to ex-

164

tend my tour here for another year, and they're promoting me to colonel!"

Normally, the news would have been a cause for celebration. The colonelship brought higher pay and--more importantly--additional privileges, with access to special vacations on the Black Sea and the promise of a dacha, or country house, when he retired. Although she imagined marrying the man, Marina wasn't impressed. She sat in sullen silence, gazing down into a glass of cheap Moldovan wine.

Never patient, Boris exploded in anger. "What's the fucking problem?" he shouted. "Aren't you happy for me?"

Marina was a tough and fearless woman, the daughter of a famous Russian explorer who died during an Arctic expedition.

"Sure, Boris, I'm happy for you, but I'm sad for us. I'm leaving, in three months, to work at the Scientific Research Institute for Infectious Diseases in Kiev. They're sending me overseas next year, to spread Communism and bestow the benefits of socialist medicine on the poor people of Africa." The tone of Marina's voice conveyed the contempt she felt for the Soviet system and the corrupt leadership of the Communist Party.

Boris was stunned, but instead of asking her to change her mind, to marry him, he tried to bully her into submission.

"You're not going anywhere!" he hissed. "Don't forget, I have to clear every assignment in and out of this place. All I have to do is to place a note in your file, documenting your anti-Soviet statements, and the next thing you know, you'll find yourself researching infectious diseases at a mining camp somewhere above the Arctic circle!"

Boris knew Marina's father died in the Arctic, and everyone knew syphilis was the most common disease in Siberian mining camps, so he realized his words would sting. He didn't know how badly his words would come back to hurt him in the end.

"You bastard!" Marina muttered. "Don't you care what's going on around you? Don't you know we're developing weapons here, with one purpose: to kill millions, indiscriminately, old men, women, even children? I'm sick of it, Boris, and I refuse to be a part of this any more!"

"Shhh!" he whispered, genuinely afraid someone might overhear Marina's words, treasonous words that could ruin him, too, if he failed to report them first.

"Shut your fucking mouth, before I shut it for you!" Boris leaned forward, his face flushed and his fists clenched. Most of the time in his relations with Marina, Boris was polite, even charming. When he was angry, however, he behaved as his father did when he returned from the war in Germany.

"Do your worst!" Marina responded through clenched teeth, as she stood and slapped Boris hard across the face.

For 20 years, Boris had blamed himself for not following Marina out that door, for failing to find her in the desert, for failing to beg her forgiveness, and for failing to save her.

Shaking off the painful memory as best he could, Boris worked his way through the tangle of debris to the main stairway and slowly climbed six flights of stairs.

His old office was on the top floor, just down the hall from the Commandant. As the KGB's top man on base, Boris had been responsible for safeguarding some of the Soviet Union's most precious secrets: the existence and capabilities of its most dangerous biological weapons. Those had been the best days of his life, a time when he never doubted his purpose or his capabilities, when he was respected by his country and his comrades, and had known love.

As he stood by the window and gazed out over the square, Boris pulled his service pistol from the holster under his arm and shot himself in the head. When the pilots found his body, his corpse was already cold.

Chapter 29: The Wild, Wild East

Martin's captors released him near the main train station in Bratislava, Slovakia, the day after Fatima returned to Tehran. His captors were considerate enough to return his belongings, which included an impressive collection of heavy gold coins sewn into his backpack. That eliminated the possibility that the men who held him were from Russia or Eastern Europe.

Within an hour, Martin managed to convert several coins into cash at an inflated rate fueled by a panicked commodity market and the falling dollar. He used some of the money to purchase a visa from an Azeri consular officer in Bratislava, along with a ticket to Baku on Azerbaijani Airways. The trip was risky-very risky-- but he had to get Fatima out of Iran.

At first, Martin had planned to turn himself in at the American embassy in Vienna, to make sure his former colleagues knew about the planned Al-Qaeda attacks, along with the rest of the information Fatima was able to provide. By the time he was released, however, it was clear Fatima's information had already been forwarded by his captors, based on a quick survey of the latest news reports.

"It must have been the Israelis, then," Martin thought to himself.

Freed from this obligation, and not willing to risk arrest and detention for playing so far out of bounds, Martin turned his attention to a strictly personal matter. Using a local internet cafe, Martin reactivated one of his former Iranian agents, an ethnic Kurd Martin recruited during several visits to Turkey. The middled-aged man owned a small trucking company and earned a tidy profit shipping goods back and forth across Iran's north-western borders.

The agent, codenamed "Convoy," owed everything to Martin, including his personal rig with the hidden compartment in the back of the cab. Although the compartment was large enough to conceal a person in relative safety during a border crossing, the interior looked and felt like a coffin and Martin shivered at the thought of riding in it himself.

When Martin arrived at the airport in Baku, he hired a driver to show him around town. After sizing up the young man and concluding he wasn't dangerous, Martin asked if he could help him find private lodgings for the week, since local hotels were too expensive and the food was terrible. Based on his previous experience traveling in the region, Martin knew many cash-strapped Azeris were eager to earn a little extra on the side. Some families actually let out their entire apartment, on a short-term basis, whenever an opportunity presented itself.

"Of course, Mister, you can stay at my sister's place. She has a very clean apartment in the Inner City, in the same building as our mother, so she can move back home with us for the week. Her husband died last year, so she could use the money. Our mother is a wonderful cook. She'll prepare as many meals as you like, for a small fee."

Fortunately for Martin, there were still enough European-looking men in Baku to allow him to blend in without too much effort. He spoke excellent Russian, with a Baltic accent, which wasn't all that unusual, especially when spoken by a man wearing a Latvian-made jacket purchased at a local shop.

The city had become a crossroads of sorts, a former provincial capitol of the Czarist and Soviet empires that somehow morphed into a bustling center of international intrigue. Pipelines were the name of the game: billions of dollars in pipelines needed to pump oil and natural gas from Kazakhstan and Turkmenistan to thirsty markets in Western Europe.

The Azeri security service was still dangerous, of course, but they were too busy collecting their share of the windfall to pay much attention to an insignificant foreigner who kept his head down and avoided the most notorious nightspots. A roving Irishman would be regarded as more of a target of opportunity for scam artists than a threat to Azeri national security.

And so it was with Martin. He left the apartment only when necessary and spoke only when spoken to. On the second day, he made contact with Convoy in the courtyard of an anonymous apartment block, next to a dry, crumbling fountain made of cheap concrete during the Soviet era.

"Well, my brother," Convoy grumbled, with a sense of irony. "I didn't expect to see you again, unless the fan was about to hit the shit." Convoy spoke excellent English and took pride in his ability to use American slang.

"I see your powers of prediction are as awe-inspiring as ever," Martin joked.

"Yes," Convoy responded and nodded his head, "as soon as I saw the news on television, I knew you would have need. But the deal is off if you start dropping bombs. Don't get me wrong, I couldn't care less if your new President kills that madman Ahmadinejad and all the mullahs--good riddance! But I won't be happy if you blow up my warehouse or my trucks!"

"I understand, my friend," Martin responded. "This is a one-time deal. I need you to smuggle someone out of Tehran. You can bring her here, to Baku, yourself. I'll give you half the payment in gold today and the rest when you return."

Convoy held out his hand and accepted the gold coins from Martin. "A woman, you say. That's interesting. I suppose she could pose as my wife, if she's willing!" Martin cringed at the thought as he examined Convoy's black and broken teeth through thin lips framed by a coarse beard.

"She's much too old for you, my friend, so please save yourself for a young Ukranian prostitute here in Baku!" Martin joked, hoping to conceal his personal interest in Fatima.

"Have one of your sons deliver this letter, unopened, to the lady at this address in Tehran," Martin continued. "The letter should be delivered at 10 in the morning on a workday. She will follow the directions I've given to find your warehouse. She'll show up sometime between seven and eight that evening. You'll need to leave for the border immediately. Do you remember the proper procedures for the crossing?"

"Of course, of course! I've practiced everything, even after you sent me the message and told me to stay cooled. I'll deliver the lady to you safely, I promise. After that, you're on your own." Convoy frowned and stood a bit taller, so Martin would take him more seriously.

"Thank you, my friend. After this, your debt to me will be paid in full. I would suggest, of course, that you avoid parking your trucks anywhere near a government facility when you get back to Tehran!" Martin suggested, only half in jest.

"To be sure, my friend, to be sure!"

The two men said their goodbyes and Convoy left to deliver his load of pomegranates to a German-owned food processing plant on the outskirts of Baku. Pomegranate juice was the latest health craze in Europe and the price was higher than ever.

"Too bad the filthy bastards working at the plant never wash their hands!" Convoy mumbled to himself, as he put the gold coins in his pocket and imagined how he would spend his latest windfall.

Chapter 30: On the Brink

Ambassador Thomas Hart Benton III was a respected professional. The son of a former professor at the American University in Beirut, Benton spoke fluent Arabic and was a natural choice for such a sensitive posting. He was not without ambition and had jumped at the opportunity to establish an informal back channel with the Islamic Republic of Iran when he was approached by an intermediary shortly after his arrival in Lebanon.

The Ambassador paced nervously and wondered what the Iranian envoy wanted to talk about. Was it possible they could avert another unnecessary war?

"Mr. Ambassador, they're on their way." The Ambassador's secretary opened the door just wide enough to get his attention. "Should I send the others in?"

"Yes, Margaret, thank you, please send them in."

The dark paneled door opened wider and three Embassy officers emerged: Janet Reid, the brilliant if caustic Deputy Chief of Mission; Army Colonel Mark Tolliver, the Defense Attache and veteran of combat missions in Iraq and Afghanistan; and Todd Smith, the CIA's new Chief of Station in Beirut.

The Ambassador had an assertive leadership style:

"All right then, I want all of you to listen carefully to everything the Iranians have to say, but there will be no need for any of you to speak. We'll have a chance to discuss the meeting in private after they leave. Is that clear?"

"Yes, of course, Mr. Ambassador," Janet responded, answering for all three of his staff.

Todd Smith was relatively young to be a Chief of Station, only 35 years old, but that's the way things were in the Agency. In the old days, before the violent upheavals of the 1980s, COS Beirut was a coveted position, usually reserved for seasoned veterans. But the Agency was stretched thin by the wars in Iraq and Afghanistan and a generation of officers had retired, leaving plenty of headroom behind.

Todd was an aggressive young man and had seen some tough duty in Iraq, like most of the officers in his generation. He looked forward to meeting the Iranian Embassy delegation. Although Ambassador Benton had made it clear his counterpart, Iranian Ambassador Javad Mostaghim, was strictly off-limits, Todd hoped some other opportunity would present itself.

The Iranian Ambassador was escorted into the room a few minutes later. A tall, slim, elegant-looking man in his early fifties, Ambassador Mostaghim wore a dark suit with a banded white collar, in the Iranian style. He was accompanied by his own Deputy Chief of Mission and a First Secretary, whom Todd knew was working under cover for the Iranian Ministry of Intelligence and Security. Perfect!

Introductions were made and Todd gave his secret counterpart a friendly handshake and a knowing look, which was returned in kind.

After the usual pleasantries and coffee and tea were served, the group got down to business.

"Ambassador Mostaghim, I'm very pleased you've allowed me to host our meeting today," Ambassador

Benton began. I'm honored to be a part of our effort to improve mutual understanding between our two nations, and I assure you any message you present will reach the highest levels of our government."

A professional diplomat himself, Ambassador Mostaghim had no idea his government was involved in a plot to help Al-Qaeda acquire weapons of mass destruction. The idea was unthinkable, and he assumed the entire mess was just another ploy by the Americans and their Zionist friends, intended to threaten and intimidate his country. Even after the terrible bombings in Russia, Iraq and the United States, the Ambassador never considered the possibility that his own government might be culpable.

As a result, he was pleased when he was asked to deliver a message of condolence from the Iranian people, along with a very considerable gift for the American government:

"Thank you, Ambassador Benton. I am also honored to participate in this meeting and I hope our efforts will lead to a deescalation of current tensions and perhaps a little more understanding in the future."

"First, allow me to begin by expressing the heartfelt condolences of the Iranian people for the victims of the attack on your sovereign territory. There is no excuse for such an act of barbarity and my government has already issued a public condemnation. Having been brutally invaded by Saddam's army during our long war with Iraq, the Iranian people understand better than most what it means to be violated in such a manner."

Ambassador Mostaghim raised the issue of the Iran-Iraq war deliberately, since everyone knew the U.S.

Government had supported Saddam's aggression at the time.

"Secondly, I am authorized by my government to offer our complete cooperation in tracking down the perpetrators.   As you know, the leaders of Al-Qaeda have claimed responsibility; speaking for ourselves, we take them at their word."

"As proof of our sincerity, I am authorized to inform you that my government is actively searching for any members of Al-Qaeda who may be hiding, illegally, within our borders.   I understand we have already arrested one man, Usama Bin Laden's son Awwab Bin Laden, who was captured as he tried to enter our country using a false Pakistani passport. My subordinate, First Secretary Bayat, is authorized to make arrangements to fly Awwab to the international airport of your choosing, where he will be turned over to the appropriate American authorities."

Todd couldn't believe his luck: he would be the only CIA officer in the world involved in a direct liaison relationship with an Iranian intelligence officer, a relationship that was already guaranteed to produce spectacular results: Awwab Bin Laden, no less, a true high-value target!

"Secondly, as a supreme gesture of goodwill and mark of our sincerity, I am authorized to present the following document, which provides detailed information on the location of Usama Bin Laden and his top lieutenants. Several safehouses in Pakistan have been identified by our highly competent intelligence services and the maps are quite detailed. Of course, my government will deny having provided this information, should it be leaked to the public. That said, we would understand completely if your government felt compelled to use the information immediately, to bring justice to the men who committed this atrocity."

"Finally, and most importantly, I am authorized to advise your government that there are absolutely no weapons of mass destruction within the borders of the Islamic Republic of Iran. If we find any illegal weapons within our borders, they will be seized immediately and your government will be informed."

"May I suggest, with all due respect, Mr. Ambassador, that the United States look outside Iran when searching for those responsible for the latest terrorist attacks on your country. I think we can agree the weapons are Russian, so look to them for an explanation. I also think we can agree Al-Qaeda was responsible for planning the attacks. For our part, the Government of Iran has done and will continue to do everything in its power to help your government bring these evil men to justice."

"All we ask, in return, is a public acknowledgment that the Government of Iran has responded in a helpful manner to your President's request for assistance. In addition, we would be grateful if your government will show some restraint and silence those irresponsible men calling for an unjust war. Surely the American people have no interest in such a thing? Your economy is already suffering from a serious recession, which has also hurt my country, and your people are still bearing the cost of two wars on our eastern and western borders."

Ambassador Benton had been waiting all his life for this opportunity: a chance to avert war, to use diplomacy to advance America's interests, without the need for bloodshed. Although the Ambassador admired and respected his colleagues in the military, he resented the dominant role the Pentagon gained over U.S. foreign policy during the Bush administration. He sincerely hoped the Iranian initiative would provide momentum for the kind of change envisioned by President Obama.

Like every American, the Ambassador wanted his government to find and punish the men responsible for the deaths of so many innocent people, but he didn't want his country to go to war with Iran based on a single, raw intelligence report. Ambassador Benton had been around long enough to know human intelligence, like the people it came from, was often flawed.

Feeling hopeful and energized, Ambassador Benton rose from his chair to shake his Iranian counterpart's hand:

"Mr. Ambassador, I'm confident my government will be deeply moved by the condolences and tangible expressions of goodwill you offered during our meeting today. I can assure you I'll do everything in my power to ensure the tone and substance of our discussions receives the attention it deserves in Washington. In the meantime, may I suggest we plan to meet once a week, to preserve the momentum you've generously begun?"

"We will see, Ambassador Benton, we will see."

The Iranian hoped he would be able to accept the invitation, but he would need further guidance from Tehran. And of course, everything depended on the American response. He knew his country was very close to war, and it saddened him to know that some members of his government wouldn't be entirely disappointed if the U.S. attacked.

The post-meeting discussion led by Ambassador Benton was brief. All three of his senior staffers had immediate cables and e-mails to write. In the meantime, the Ambassador had a few telephone calls to make.

"Margaret, get Secretary Clinton on the line immediately."

On his way out the door, Colonel Tolliver tugged on Todd Smith's sleeve and pulled him aside for a private conversation.

"Do you think the Iranians are serious?" he asked.

"We'll know soon enough," Todd responded. "When it comes to Persians, you have to assume they're playing some kind of a game. "It's in my nature," as the scorpion said to the frog. They can't help themselves. But if they deliver Awwab Bin Laden to us on a silver platter, and if the information on UBL's location is accurate, who cares? Let's bomb the shit out of Al-Qaeda and sort things out when the dust settles."

"I'm sure the Air Force and the Navy already have enough resources in place--the only thing they need is targeting data, and we can provide that," the Colonel said. "I'll fax my copy of the Iranian document to the Pentagon immediately. Now, don't you Langley boys go scaring Usama away with your puny Predators--let's leave this one for the big boys."

"Hell, Colonel, you know that decision is way above my pay grade. But I can tell you my headquarters will kill me if they don't get a copy of this document right away!"

The two men exchanged a grim look before racing off to their respective offices.

Six hours after the two Americans reported back to Washington, pilotless Predator aircraft circled above two of the safehouses identified in the document. One of the compounds appeared to have been recently abandoned; the second was occupied and a pair of Toyota pickup trucks were visible just inside a crumbling mud brick stable with a makeshift, camoflagued roof. Several armed men were busy covering the trucks with tarps, and a group of at least 10 other men were observed walking up a steep trail towards the entrance to a cave.

Meanwhile, Usama Bin Laden sat in a circle on a large Afghan rug with six of his most trusted companions. It was morning and the sun shone brightly, providing illumination for their work just inside the cave. Bin Laden's companions were nervous as they described the results of the attack on Orlando. The somber, bearded leader didn't bother to hide his disappointment as the young men explained why the nuclear attack planned for New York or Washington had failed. Eager to please the man who inspired him, a portable DVD player with excerpts from recent cable news broadcasts was carefully placed on a low table in front of Bin Laden. The great man seemed distracted at first as he stared at the screen and stroked his long beard, but his eyes lit up quickly when he witnessed the scenes of death and destruction.

"God has willed it!" he uttered, as he turned to address his supporters. "Our sacred martyrs have struck a deadly blow, cutting out the heart of the enemy!"

At that moment, a command was issued from the far side of the world and several Predators launched a coordinated attack on the cave and the nearby compound. A lucky shot with a Hellfire missile caused the cave to collapse, killing Usama Bin Laden and six of his supporters instantly. Months later, their bodies were recovered by the Taliban and buried in secret.

Within the hour, a massive airstrike leveled the other safehouses identified by the Iranians, with quite a few Taliban strongholds thrown in for good measure. Surrounding villages were also targeted and any vehicles moving in or out of the target zones were destroyed.

In the process, Al-Qaeda ceased to exist as an organization with any form of central control. It survived in cyberspace, in websites dedicated to the memory of lost heros, and in the imaginations of young jihadists who continued to operate in small but dangerous groups all over the world.

The legacy was strongest in Pakistan, where a group of coup plotters took advantage of the general population's outrage in reaction to the latest American assault on their sovereignty. With a little planning and a great deal of money in the right hands, a series of violent protests were organized. In part due to civil strife associated with the global recession, the Pakistani government was quickly overthrown and the country fell into a bloody civil war, with the Army split between supporters of the Taliban and the President's remaining loyalists, led by the Army Chief of Staff.

Three days after Pakistan rejected an offer from the Americans and their British allies to secure its nuclear arsenal on ships off the coast, a half-dozen air-deliverable nuclear bombs were seized during a daring raid led by a deeply religious Pakistani officer with close ties to the Taliban leadership.

A week later, one of the stolen bombs was used in a nuclear strike on an important Indian Army base in the disputed territory of Kashmir, in an effort to draw support for the rebels from the rest of Pakistani society by uniting the entire population in a conflict with India.

Unwilling to risk any additional nuclear attacks on its territory and having no way of knowing how many weapons the Pakistani rebels controlled, the Indian Government launched a preemptive strike, not only on the rebels' known positions, but also on Pakistan's entire nuclear infrastructure.

Thus began the Great Indo-Pakistani War, which left millions dead and chaos in its wake. Although India eventually won the war, the country lost its long struggle with sectarianism as the Muslim minority turned against the majority Hindu government. Thousands of Muslim men felt they had no choice, after their wives and children were slaughtered and their homes were burned to the ground by violent opportunists from Hindu nationalist parties. To avoid outright civil war, the world's largest democracy was forced to declare martial law.

Chapter 31: Family Affairs

When Colonel Sattar Fakoor arrived home from work a bit earlier than usual, he surprised his wife, Fatima, as she was packing a small bag in their bedroom.

"Where in the hell do you think you're going?" he demanded.

With years of experience, Fatima had learned how to manipulate her husband, at least some of the time. One of the first lessons she learned was to avoid escalating a confrontation, while projecting an air of self-confidence. Her husband was the worst kind of bully and his aggressive instincts were ignited when he sensed fear or weakness.

"Oh, hello, husband--what a pleasure to have you home so early in the evening," she responded. "I'm just packing a bag so I can stay with your mother at the hospital tonight. I stopped by to see her this morning and she begged me to sleep over. She has some minor surgery scheduled for tomorrow morning. You remember, they need to remove that little rod from her forearm?" Fatima waited for her husband to respond.

"Yes, yes, of course. How is she doing?" Sattar asked.

"The break is healing well," Fatima continued. "The doctor said she should be able to come home in a couple of days, but your mother is scared and asked me to stay, to help look after her."

His anger somewhat deflated, Sattar responded gruffly:

"Well, I suppose I should visit her tomorrow morning after the surgery. Call me at the office when she's back in her room and I'll stop by, if I can."

The couple's conversation was interrupted by a distinctive ringing sound coming from the special telephone in Sattar's study. When he picked up the receiver, he heard the front door close and he wondered for a moment why Fatima was leaving for the hospital so soon, without preparing his dinner. Before he could think things over, his attention was diverted by the General's voice on the other end of his phone:

"Colonel, I want you to contact your man Ali Kalbasi immediately. We've just received a report that Awwab Bin Laden has crossed the border from Pakistan. I assume he's heading for Kalbasi's compound in Zahedan. Tell Kalbasi he must place Awwab under protective custody immediately."

"Yes, of course, General. Are we really going to turn him over to the Americans?" Sattar asked.

"Of course not, you idiot. I've arranged a special flight for you at 0600 tomorrow morning. I want you to make all of the arrangements and I will hold you personally responsible. Awwab must be executed, and it must look like he was shot while attempting to escape. Put his body on ice and we'll give that to the Americans. Be sure to leave enough remains for a DNA test. We don't want to disappoint the Americans."

"Let me make myself clear," the General continued. "Kalbasi has grown too close to Awwab, so don't leave this operation to him. Our link with Al-Qaeda must be severed, cleanly and completely. Do you understand?"

184

"Yes, General, it will be done as you command."

After placing the receiver back on the telephone, Sattar paced in his study for a few minutes, preparing a plan of action. He decided he'd better visit his mother at the hospital as soon as he finished packing for his trip, since he wouldn't be able to pay his respects after her surgery in the morning. Perhaps he should take Fatima out for dinner, to reward her for being such a dutiful daughter-in-law?

As he drove toward the hospital an hour later, Sattar mused about his wife. She had been strangely compliant since her return from Vienna and had not objected when he took her the first evening. Although she wasn't as young as she used to be, Sattar still enjoyed the feeling of power he held over a beautiful woman from a prestigious family.

Fatima was an infuriating mystery, to be sure. Sattar knew she didn't love him and had only agreed to marry him in order to protect her father, an arrogant academic who looked to the West instead of his own culture, his own religion, to solve Iran's problems. The old man would have been out there in the streets with all the other protestors, if he had lived to see the last presidential election, that's for sure. But Sattar's life with Fatima had been much better than he expected, until their son died. She was the one who encouraged their son to pursue gymnastics, a sport favored by Tehran's elite families, rather than soccer, his sport, the sport of working-class men.

Sattar's heart sank as unwanted images of his beautiful son flashed before his eyes. After parking his car in the parking lot behind the hospital, Sattar rested his forehead on the steering wheel and rubbed his eyes with the palms of his hands. Distracted by the sound of an ambulance, Sattar pulled himself together and walked toward the main entrance.

When he arrived at his mother's private room in a modern hospital, a special privilege she enjoyed as the son of a senior Guards officer, he was surprised to find his mother alone.

"Hello, Mother, where's Fatima?"

"Oh, that wife of yours came by this morning and left some flowers," the old woman responded as she nodded toward a small vase on the windowsill. "When are you going to get that woman under control? She's much too independent; imagine, flying off to Europe for a shopping trip! If she had done her duty and given you more children, she wouldn't be so much trouble!"

"Wait, Mother, I saw her at home, just a few minutes ago. She said she was on her way here, to spend the night with you, to help you recover from your surgery in the morning!"

"What are you talking about, son? I told her this morning the surgery was delayed until the end of this week. My arm is still knitting and the doctors don't want to rush things..."

Before his mother could finish her thought, Sattar rushed out the door and ran toward his car. Why had Fatima lied to him? Where was she going? Where did she think she could hide?

When Sattar reached his car, he was hit with a sudden realization. The leak--it had to be Fatima! She was the only person in his circle who had been out of the country! Then his mind began to grasp the implications: General Suleimani didn't know his wife had trav-

186

eled to Vienna and he certainly didn't know about her Lebanese friend. Sure, the General's family benefitted as much as anyone else from the system of gift-giving by privileged subordinates, but he would suspect Fatima immediately if he knew about her recent travel. Praise Allah, Sattar had not yet presented the gift Fatima purchased for the General's wife!

Although he wasn't an intellectual, like his wife, Sattar was blessed with a quick and clever mind, and it only took a moment to assess the situation. There was one way he could save himself: he had to find Fatima! To do that, he would need help from the Revolutionary Guard.

Thirty minutes later, Sattar stood at attention on the private veranda of General Suleiani's ostentatious house in Farmanieh, one of north Tehran's most prestigious neighborhoods.

"General, I believe I have discovered the source of the leak," Sattar struggled to explain.

"Well, out with it, Colonel!" The General knew Sattar to be one of his most ruthless and ambitious subordinates. He assumed Sattar was prepared to identify one of his rivals as the source of the leak.

"It's my wife, Fatima, General." Sattar cringed, as he anticipated his boss's reaction.

"What!" the General roared. "Explain yourself!"

"General, I throw myself on your mercy, and the mercy of Allah. She must have overheard our private conversation at my home several weeks ago. I thought she was sleeping, but that's the only way she could have known. I swear, I never discussed the operation with her!"

The General's rage moderated when he realized he shared some responsibility for the leak - all the more reason to resolve the problem before anyone found out. That chain of thought lead to other questions that needed answers:

"Yes, yes, I see how she might have heard more than she should have. But why would she leak the information, and to whom? I thought you brought that wife of yours under control after her father died all those years ago!"

The General was familiar with Fatima's family situation and had given Sattar credit for preventing the famous Dr. Lavasani from becoming an outspoken critic of the Islamic Republic when he first returned from America. In fact, Sattar's clever manipulations sowed the seeds for what had been a very successful career with the Revolutionary Guards.

"General, it is my duty to report that I allowed my wife to travel to Vienna on a shopping trip. The news about our sensitive operation broke just before she returned. It must have been her. With your permission, General, I will lead the search so she can be brought in for questioning."

"What search? Isn't she at home, where she belongs?" The General stood within inches of Sattar's face and glared into the shorter man's eyes. "I thought your had that woman under control, after she was seen at one of those unlawful demonstrations after the election?"

"General, it shames me to report my wife disappeared a few hours ago. She told me she was planning to stay at the hospital with my mother--you may remember she had a nasty fall? But that was a lie."

"Yes, now I understand your shame. But I cannot allow you to lead the search--you must leave the first thing tomorrow morning for Zahedan, as planned. No, I will take care of this problem for you, and if Fatima confesses, as surely she will, then you, at least, will live to serve Allah a bit longer."

"Thank you, General, I won't fail you." Sattar lowered his head and left the house quickly, grateful to have survived, for now, and determined to handle the problem in Zahedan without disappointing the General. He felt a pang of regret for Fatima's likely fate but quickly pushed the thought aside.

Within the hour, a order was issued to arrest Fatima on sight. Photographs and special instructions were distributed at every police station and border crossing, to make sure Fatima was intercepted if she tried to leave the country. The General was confident his subordinates would find Fatima quickly. After all, where could a mere woman hide?

At that moment, Fatima was taking the first of five cab rides across the great city of Tehran, trying to make sure no one was following her before she showed up at the the address provided by the unexpected messenger. She felt awkward but determined, and imagined she wouldn't go wrong if she tried to imitate the multi-stage journey she had taken across Vienna.

Martin's message was brief but clear:

"Dear F. I hope this note finds you safe and well. I'll be waiting for you when you reach the end of your journey, with transportation provided by a friend. Suggest you pack a small overnight bag and take a tour of the city before you arrive at my friend's address between seven and eight this evening. Someday I hope to earn the trust you've given me. Love, M."

The route Fatima took was random, at first, but became more deliberate with each cab ride. She didn't look back when she left her husband's home in the Shahrak-e Gharb district, in the northwestern quarter of the city. It didn't take long to find her first cab, which quickly carried her to a busy shopping area with multiple entrances. When she first took her seat in a second cab, she was momentarily at a loss for words, until her next destination passed her lips, seemingly of its own volition.

Fatima sat quietly as she floated in a dream, reliving her idyllic childhood in the Niavaran district. Her heart jumped as her taxi passed through Tajrish Square and her mind flooded with memories of happier times. The elegant homes and prestigious apartment buildings lining Darband Street seemed to drift by as the cab floated up a gentle slope toward Niavaran park.

Fatima cherished her childhood memories. Her mother and father were loving parents and never allowed their busy careers to interfere with their family life. Her mother was a well-known artist, a painter with an effortless manner who seemed to bring her well-dressed daughter to every cultural event in the city. All of her mother's friends were talented, educated, inspiring women, with smiles on their faces and wisdom to share. Fatima still missed her mother, several decades after her death, and couldn't have imagined the person she would have become without her memory.

Fatima's thoughts turned to her father as she stepped out of her cab at the entrance to Niavaran Park. Their shared grief at the death of her mother bound them tightly together. Her father was a respected professor at the University of Tehran, with many responsibilities, none of which he took more seriously than his daughter. Fatima retraced one of their favorite walks, on foot and in her memory, past the amphitheater, museum and music hall, with a stop at the Cafe Gallerie, as she admired the sparkling fountains and lush gardens. She remembered the summer days of her childhood, the hours at her mother's side in the Farhangsara, or Art House, and the long afternoons in the comfortable library.

The climate was much cooler in Niavarn than the rest of the city, and Fatima would never forget those perfect mornings, when the sky was crisp and clean and every cell in her young body felt alive. She took a deep breath and tried to recall that feeling, to be 12 years old and a picture of health, but her mood changed suddenly when a cloud passed overhead and her steps carried her to a darker place.

Fatima kept walking for another half hour until she reached a small cemetery where her family were buried. Her son lay next to the grandparents he'd never met. Fatima knew her mother and father would have been proud of Omid and she hoped they would meet in the afterlife.

As a young woman, Fatima was a religious skeptic and, like her father, had always allowed her intellectual side to dominate. After suffering real pain in her life, she became more like her mother and believed she would have to invent God, if he didn't exist. The thought that her mother, her father and her son might be lost forever was just too much to bear. The thought that she might live the rest of her own life without hope, without purpose, was just as painful.

When Fatima finally stood up, she knew it was time to go. With growing resolve, she bid a final farewell and turned her back on the past, even as she relied on her memories to sustain her faith in the future.

Chapter 32: The Road to Freedom

It was four in the morning and the desert sky was a black velvet curtain that rose and sank over the glare of on-coming traffic. Fatima sat on the bench behind Convoy as he drove west, toward the Iranian border with Azer-baijan. She wore a full burkha, head to toe, in Afghan style. If the truck was stopped, she would remain silent and play the role of a humble truck driver's wife. Her disguise was enhanced by the fact that no Iranian po-liceman would ever speak directly to a woman accom-panied by her husband. Although her situation was grim, Fatima laughed out loud when she realized she had finally found an advantage to being a woman in the Islamic Republic of Iran.

Convoy glanced back at Fatima but didn't ask why she was laughing. Having no idea who she might be, he was understandably nervous and sensed trouble. From the first moment she opened her mouth at his ware-house outside Tehran, he recognized her for what she was: an educated, upper-class woman, probably well-connected, undoubtedly missed by powerful men.

While fumbling with his radio and glancing in his mirrors, Convoy reviewed his options. He briefly con-sidered the possibility of killing the woman and dump-ing her body in the desert, but he had no experience with murder and would probably make a mess of it. And there was the reward, of course, enough money to expand his business so he could leave a lasting legacy for his sons and his grandchildren.

Convoy resolved to keep his commitment, as long as the American kept his. Surely the gain was worth the risk? After all, he thought he would have to make several such border crossings, when he first accepted Martin's proposal.

As the truck rumbled along the bumpy, two-lane highway, Convoy spotted a landmark that required him to make his final preparations. They were getting close to the border and he needed to find a quiet spot where they were unlikely to attract attention.

As he pulled to the shoulder, Convoy spoke briefly to Fatima:

"It's time. Please move to the front passenger seat while I get everything ready."

Convoy couldn't avoid noticing Fatima's graceful neck and narrow waist as she climbed over the center console. Although he saw himself as a modern man, not like those idiots in the religious police, Convoy had never been alone with a beautiful woman before; he was disappointed in himself for feeling uncomfortable, and acted gruffly in response.

With a few quick motions, Convoy released the hidden latch that enabled him to lift the rear bench high enough to reveal a secret compartment hidden beneath the floor. Convoy remembered how amazed he had been when Martin first showed him the compartment, shortly after he accepted delivery of the beautiful Volvo tractor-trailer cab in Turkey. From the outside, no one could imagine there might be enough space to conceal a grown man, or a woman. The compartment was sealed and climate controlled, to prevent any fumes from flowing in and to prevent any trace of a human presence from leaking out.

Martin told Convoy how the Volvo's sheet metal had been specially formed, to make it look like any other Volvo truck, but with slightly different dimensions that yielded just enough space to hide a man in a prone position. The compartment was lined with padded brown leather and was equipped with a handful of LED lights so the occupant could operate his own climate controls and oxygen supply, enough for 8-10 hours. The compartment also had held a few bottles of water and a relief tube designed for use by a male passenger; the builders never imagined the concealment would ever be used by a woman.

Convoy explained the system to Fatima as she looked over his shoulder. He drew a privacy curtain over the window when he noticed another truck approaching from behind. When that truck slowed and passed without stopping, Fatima pulled back her veil and spoke quietly: "I suppose I had better answer nature's call before you lock me in this thing." She offered Convoy a smile--after all, she was entrusting him with her life.

"Yes, yes, of course," Convoy responded with embarrassment. "Can you climb down by yourself?"

"I think I can manage!" Fatima responded, as she opened the passenger door and climbed nimbly down to street level.

Convoy turned on his radio and sat in the driver's seat, to offer his passenger a semblance of privacy.

For the first time since she was a little girl on a camping trip with her father, Fatima relieved herself by squatting at the side of the road. She gazed out toward the empty desert and the canopy of stars, much more alive than they appeared in the city. Rising to adjust her clothing, Fatima prayed that she would live to see the stars again.

When Fatima was very young, before her family fled the Shah's secret police, she was locked in the truck of an abandoned car by two of her playmates. She panicked at the time and had cried for over an hour until she was rescued by her mother. With the fear of confined spaces still present in her mind, Fatima wondered if she would be brave enough to survive the rest of the journey, or strong enough to start a new life.

For a moment Fatima found it difficult to identify the feeling, but she realized she wanted to live; she had a reason to live, for the first time since her son died. Determined to do her part, Fatima climbed back into the cab.

"All right, I'm ready," she stated flatly, as she removed her Afghan-style burkha and dusty shoes and tossed them into the secret compartment before climbing in herself, feet first.

"Don't worry, Madame, I've tested it myself. Everything works fine and you've got more than enough air to last the entire trip, two times over. There, get comfortable. Do you see the light switch? Go ahead and turn that on before I seal everything up. Okay, here goes."

Fatima lay quietly in the coffin-size compartment and closed her eyes in an effort to calm herself. The padded leather surface was quite comfortable, like a fine sofa, and her burkha made a serviceable pillow.

Fatima's thoughts were disjointed, as if she didn't know herself any more. The years since her return to

Tehran seemed so unreal. First, she lost her father, and for a time she couldn't imagine how she would go on living, married to a man she despised, feeling like she didn't belong, as the Islamic Republic of Iran began to take shape.

But then, less than a year after her father's death, Allah blessed Fatima with a child, a beautiful boy, and she felt alive. For reasons she would never understand, her only child was taken from her, and she had struggled with painful depression for two years. She had a few close friends and tried to stay busy, tutoring their children in French and English, but the sight of her son's former classmates was hard to take.

Her days had been dark, but at least she had some time alone now, with herself. The nights had been darker still and she flinched when she recalled the beatings. The first time Fatima resisted sex, her husband left her battered and bruised, unable to leave the house. The beatings weren't frequent, but the sense of humiliation was long-lasting. She had given up hope, for a time, and still found it hard to believe she might actually escape.

Fatima's thoughts were interrupted by a bump and jolt as the truck ground to a halt. Fatima didn't know it, but Convoy's truck was standing at the end of a long line of traffic that extended four kilometers back from the border with Azerbaijan. Special security measures were being taken on the Iranian side of the border, and it might be hours before Convoy's truck reached the checkpoint.

Chapter 33: Operation Just Avenger

The U.S. military learned a great deal during the conflicts in Iraq and Afghanistan. In a time of war, when the consequences of poor leadership were most apparent, the armed forces evolved into a true meritocracy. The same process was observed in every great American war, as weaker knives were broken on the grindstone of battle and the sharpest leaders emerged. As a result, officers with skills honed in two difficult wars were chosen to plan and execute Operation Just Avenger, a complex, coordinated effort to destroy Iran's ability to produce or deploy weapons of mass destruction. This objective presupposed another task: the Islamic Republic's ability to defend its strategic assets also had to be eliminated.

A vast array of assets was deployed to achieve this mission, as ordered by the Commander in Chief. The first wave of attacks destroyed 90 percent of Iran's functional fighter aircraft and 75 percent of its surface-to-air missile systems, along with command and control facilities. A second wave using both bombers and cruise missiles destroyed every known Revolutionary Guards objective in the country, including headquarters buildings, subordinate offices in regional cities, and remote bases used for training insurgents. Quds Force commander General Suleimani was killed in one of those attacks.

Although most of the Guards' facilities were empty and their personnel dispersed to safer locations, the leadership's ability to direct its resources was disrupted, at least for a time. The second wave also targeted Iranian naval assets and missile units deployed on the Persian Gulf.

The third wave of attacks leveled every fixed objective associated with Iran's nuclear program. Specially-developed munitions featuring technologies further refined after the initial air attacks on Iraq in 2002 were used to destroy all of Iran's deep underground facilities--even those that were not known to be involved in the nuclear program--because they could be used to shelter a secret program in the future.

Militarily and tactically, Operation Just Avenger achieved its objectives. Iran's nuclear program suffered a serious setback and would take years to recover. Its ability to project military power to threaten or intimidate U.S. allies in the region was severely degraded. Most particularly, Iran's ability to use traditional military assets to threaten U.S. naval forces and oil shipments in the Persian Gulf was all but eliminated.

Politically and strategically, the operation was a disaster. The Iranian people rose up in opposition to the latest American aggression and any remaining internal dissidents were silenced. As a result, the Iranian Islamic Revolution was strengthened and survived for another 40 years. The Government of Iran was more determined than ever to acquire nuclear weapons and would eventually succeed, in part because international support for the U.S. Government's counterproliferation policies collapsed after the Great Indo-Pakistani War and the U.S. attacks on Iran. Petty dictatorships and wobbly democratic governments alike reached the same conclusion: they had no choice but to develop a nuclear deterrent of their own.

Other consequences were also severe but no less predictable. Spurred on by Iranian surrogates, Iraq dissolved into a brutal civil war. Atrocities committed by all sides in the contest exceeded the worst expectations, and expectations were already low, based on previous experience.

The Kurds were the first to declare independence, which prompted an immediate invasion by Turkey, having lost confidence in America's ability to protect its vital national interests.   A pro-Iranian Islamic Republic quickly emerged in the oil-rich, majority Shia areas, with its capitol in Basra.

Fighting erupted at every point where Shia met Sunni, and the bloodletting was far worse than anything the world had seen in 2005 or 2006.   Several Sunni groups competed for power, but it took years and numerous defeats at the hands of their Shia enemies before a single group emerged with the strength and the brutality to dominate the others.

Much of Baghdad was abandoned due to radiation poisoning in the area surrounding the Green Zone and bitter fighting in every habitable sector of the city. With no central government to protect, remaining American forces were withdrawn and a bloody civil war raged on for six more years, ending only when the country was divided into three independent states.

Within days of the U.S. attack on Iran, oil prices soared to record levels. The U.S., Asia and Western Europe slid into a deeper and longer recession. As a result, American consumers who were just beginning to open their wallets became even more cautious, and the remaining trickle of imported goods slowed to a complete stop.

Following the collapse of its export-driven economy, China retreated into xenophobia. No longer able to satisfy the rising aspirations of its people and desperate to preserve internal unity, the Chinese government staged a series of provocations that eventually led to an outright invasion of Taiwan. Most of the Chinese people rallied around the Communist Party; outspoken dissidents were rounded up and shot summarily. Badly stretched by the recession at home and the conflict in the Near East, the U.S. government was in no position to stop the invasion. Predictably, an American proposal to condemn the Chinese action was rejected by the United Nation's Security Council.

After the American attack on its territory, the Islamic government of Iran unleashed every asymmetrical resource at its disposal. Hundreds of attacks against American and Israeli targets took place during the first months, many of them carried out by Iranian-trained members of Hezbollah supported by a worldwide network of Lebanese Shia immigrants. Suicide bombers, using speed boat flotillas and operating at night, made it impossible for international corporations to insure oil tankers operating in the Persian Gulf. The poor, disadvantaged Shia populations of the Arabian peninsula rose up against their oppressors, destroying a number of oil facilities in the process.

A particularly vicious series of terrorist attacks targeted a dozen U.S. shopping malls at the height of the Christmas season. Six attacks took place on the Friday after Thanksgiving. Three of the attacks used powdered anthrax acquired by the Iranian Revolutionary Guards from sources inside Russia, causing hundreds of fatalities and overwhelming hospitals in Boston, Chicago and Atlanta. Three other attacks used small teams of suicide snipers; they managed to pick off dozens of shoppers in

Dallas, Phoenix and Miami before they were over-whelmed by the police.

Battered but not beaten, Iranian intelligence and security services used the same tactics employed in Iraq to further undermine the U.S. position in Afghanistan, already badly damaged by the fall of the pro-American government in Pakistan.

Unable to maintain control over its disaffected population without a steady flow of oil income, the Kingdom of Saudi Arabia descended into chaos. Most of the Saudi princes fled to luxurious estates in Europe. Members of the Saudi royal family who hesitated were rounded up and executed in public squares, along with hundreds of foreign infidels, many of whom were picked up at random off the streets of Riyadh and Jeddah. Since so many essential jobs were performed by foreign guest workers, the weak Saudi economy imploded. Shortly afterward, remaining U.S. forces in Saudi Arabia were withdrawn.

The flow of crude oil out of the region slowed steadily. It would take years to build enough pipeline capacity to ship the oil across the Saudi desert to Egypt, even if the country had a functioning government. By then, it would be too late, as Syria and Egypt launched another war with Israel, hoping to suppress internal dissent by rallying the people against a common enemy. The powerful Israeli Army won every battle, but they couldn't stop the rockets or the suicide bombers. Locked in a bitter stalemate, Israeli and Egyptian soldiers shelled each other across the Suez Canal, which quickly deteriorated into a stinking ditch clogged with the rusting hulks of sunken ships. Since someone had to be blamed for their repeated failures, Egyptian President

Hosni Mubarak was assassinated by his own soldiers. He was quietly replaced by a senior general with ties to the Muslim Brotherhood.

The apparent improvement in U.S.-Russian relations that followed the exchange of condolences after the terrorist attacks faded quickly. Putin's government launched a propaganda campaign intended to isolate the U.S. and identify America as a threat to international peace and security. With sources of energy in the Middle East drying up, many European nations were unwilling to antagonize their Russian suppliers. As a result, support for U.S. initiatives under the NATO umbrella dissolved. The most solicitous European countries were rewarded with special discounts on Russian oil and gas imports. Independent-minded countries were forced to pay market rates, wrecking further havoc on their economies. In some cases, internal unrest eventually led to the election of new governments with pro-Russian policies.

A few weeks after the air and missile attacks, some hard men in the upper echelons of American power argued that a ground invasion of Iran, followed by regime change, was the only way to achieve victory. During a meeting at the White House, the Secretary of Defense and the Chairman of the Joint Chiefs--well aware of the lessons learned in Iraq--rejected the idea outright, citing insufficient resources and the impossibility of occupying a country as large and populous as Iran.

Worldwide economic and financial turmoil had domestic political implications in the United States as well. A growing number of Americans embraced an isolationist agenda, and asked why a country as large as their own couldn't produce all of the goods and services it needed to replace foreign imports. When the unemployment rate reached 20 percent, hundreds of thousands of angry citizens marched in the streets and demanded an end to free trade agreements. Vigilante groups flourished along the border with Mexico, and numerous shootings were reported.

During the following winter, the coldest in 50 years, many Americans couldn't afford to buy the energy they needed to heat their homes. In fact, there wasn't enough oil or gas to go around, even if everyone could afford it. A system of rotating power outages provided some relief but not nearly enough to meet the needs of the population. Lacking employment or any other means of support, tens of thousands of people fled the Rust Belt and headed for warmer climes. The lucky ones moved in with relatives or found temporary refuge in local churches.

The Democratic administration, supported by a majority in Congress, passed emergency legislation that reminded many of programs dating back to the Great Depression: the Department of Housing and Urban Development seized thousands of homes in Florida, Texas, Arizona and Nevada that were foreclosed during the mortgage crisis and turned them into public housing units for Northern refugees. Millions of young men were channeled into public works programs, many of which were focused on alternative sources of energy.

The cost of the most useful goods and services, like solar and wind generators, skyrocketed after the collapse, as did the price of food and other commodities. Old technologies, especially internal combustion engines, were no longer desired. Hundreds of thousands of cars, trucks and SUVs with substantial liens on their titles were simply abandoned, further deepening the financial crisis and leading to the collapse of several major banks. When the price of gas reached $15 per gallon, some isolated suburban neighborhoods with no access to public transportation became ghost towns, with roaming gangs of rootless teenagers and rampant lawlessness. Special laws were passed to prevent the hoarding of food or energy. Martial law was declared in some areas and National Guard units, some of them recently back from Iraq, were deployed to keep the peace.

Chapter 34: Fatima's Fate

Convoy ran with a group of other men as they rushed toward the border with Azerbaijan. A thin line of nervous border guards used batons to shove the crowd back. Voices were raised on both sides of the line as the crowd gesticulated violently. Most of the men were truckdrivers, like Convoy. Their rigs stood still in a ragged serpentine line leading south along the Caspian Sea. Dry desert winds blew over the water, tossing brown and white foam on the rocks below. Most mornings, the border crossing was difficult and took hours to complete. Today was much worse: border guards were searching every vehicle and interviewing every passenger.

Convoy struggled to hide his panic when two guards approached and displayed a poor-quality photograph of Fatima. "Do you recognize this woman?" they wanted to know. Convoy had watched the border guards carefully as they worked their way down the long line of trucks, but he never imagined his special passenger was the subject of their interest. Throughout the morning, Convoy assumed the secret compartment would do the job and see him safely across the border; when his truck remained motionless for six hours, his confidence began to waiver.

While jogging back and forth from his truck to the border crossing for the third time, Convoy stopped suddenly when he hear the sound of a jet flying just over the horizon. Soon afterward, he heard a series of distant explosions, followed by a much closer strike on an Iranian radar installation located on a steep ridge overlooking the border. The blast caused a hail of debris to rain down on the village below, leading the terrified drivers to panic and flee to their vehicles.

Immediately after the first wave of American attacks, the officer in charge of the Iranian border crossing stood in a huddle with his dazed subordinates. One of the border guards recalled the horrifying television footage of thousands of Iraqis being slaughtered in their cars and trucks as they tried to flee Kuwait during the first Gulf War, prior to the arrival of U.S. ground forces. The Iranian commander was quickly persuaded to abandon the special security check so his fellow countrymen could resume their journey to Azerbaijan, where they would be safe.

A few moments later, the long line of trucks began to move. Sympathetic officials on the Azeribaijani side of the border waved the trucks on, as many of the drivers were ethnic Azeris like themselves. In less than an hour, Convoy's truck reached relative safety on the north side of the border.

For the first time in many years, Convoy found himself praying for the mercy of Allah; not for himself, but for the poor woman hiding in his truck. He knew the compartment had a limited supply of oxygen, and he had used more than he should when he first tested the system.

As he drove north, Convoy looked for a safe place to pull over so he could check on Fatima. He was afraid to stop too soon because an Azerbaijani government vehicle in the southbound lanes had warned the drivers to keep moving. Finally, Convoy arrived at a small service area with a gravel parking lot where he had been instructed to wait for Martin. Several other vehicles were already stopped at the same location, so he assumed they wouldn't be disturbed.

As quickly as possible, Convoy parked his rig and closed the privacy curtains he used when sleeping in the cab. He muttered a prayer as he rushed to open the latch, and cursed out loud when he pinched his fingers in the process.

No sound emerged when Convoy raised the bench and it was too dark in the back of the truck to see inside the small compartment. In a panic, he opened one of the privacy curtains just far enough to allow a splash of daylight to enter the cab. Convoy's heart sank, for the woman inside was as still and pale as a corpse, with her head resting on the burkha she had worn during the first part of their journey.

Convoy collapsed in his seat, rocking back and forth as he chanted a prayer for the dead. He thought he would die of a heart attack himself when he heard pounding and shouting at the passenger door. When he pulled up the curtain, he saw Martin standing there, demanding to be let in.

"I'm sorry!" Convoy cried out, "the lovely lady is dead! I did everything I could, but who could have known the border crossing would be closed? Allah has willed it..."

"Move out of the way!" Martin shouted, as he leapt into the cramped space behind the front seats and looked down into the compartment. As gently as possible, he gathered Fatima in his arms. Her skin was warm to the touch and he could feel a faint pulse at her neck.

"She's alive, you fool! Help me reposition the bench so she can lay down."

In a few moments, Fatima regained consciousness and awoke to find Martin's concerned face leaning over her. Her voice was weak as she whispered, "I saw you in my dreams!"

With Martin's help, Fatima managed to sit upright. Still feeling dizzy from the lack of oxygen, she took a sip from a bottle of water and brushed her hands across her face. Slowly regaining her composure, she glanced up at Martin, nodded her head weakly and said "I'm okay, I'll be okay, I promise."

Although pleased to see the woman had survived, Convoy was worried. He saw the way Martin and Fatima looked at each another and suddenly realized his American friend was involved in something unusual, something personal, something unprofessional.

"Listen to me, you bastard!" Convoy interjected. "You put both of our lives in danger! Don't you know she's a hunted woman? The Iranian border guards, the long delay, they were looking for her, don't you understand?"

Distracted and exhausted, Martin asked: "What do you mean?"

"Every driver and passenger on the Iranian side of the border was shown a photograph of this woman. They carefully searched every vehicle; that's why it was taking so long to cross the border, until you Americans started bombing and they finally let us through."

"Okay, okay!" Martin responded, while gesturing with his hands in an effort to calm Convoy down. "Give me a minute and we'll sort everything out."

"Fatima," Martin continued, "we can't stay here, we have to go. Do you think you can walk?"

"I'm still a bit dizzy, but I should be able to manage." Fatima pulled herself together and tried to adjust the Western clothes needed for travel in a secular, former Soviet republic like Azerbaijan.

"Good, let's go," Martin urged.

With some effort, Martin was able to move Fatima to the backseat of a black Volga sedan with heavily-tinted windows, a vehicle used to transport minor government officials during the Soviet era and still one of the most common vehicles on the road in all parts of the former Soviet Union. After dusting off his haggling skills, Martin had been able to purchase the car in Baku at a modestly-inflated price.

Returning quickly to Convoy's truck, Martin climbed back into the cab and spoke to his Iranian agent for the last time.

"My friend, you must believe me, I had no idea the Iranian authorities were looking for her. I'm sure you can see I would never do anything to put her life at risk. I wish I could pay you more, but this is everything I have."

Martin placed a heavy stack of Canadian maple leaf coins in Convoy's hands and closed his fist around them.

"You kept your promise, and I free you from any further obligation. I pray your family is safe in Tehran."

With his adrenaline still pumping after the dangerous border crossing, Convoy didn't speak; he simply nodded his head as he grasped Martin's hand in farewell. Convoy had always admired his American friend, but he couldn't wait to free himself from his short-lived occupation as a part-time spy.

When Martin returned to the Volga and sat behind the wheel, Fatima reached over the seat and wrapped both of her arms around the American's neck.

"I can't believe I'm free. Thank you," she said quietly.

"Fatima, it's so good to find you alive and well." Martin turned around, so he could see her more clearly.

Exhausted but greatly relieved, Fatima touched Martin's arm and asked: "What happened back there? Why were they looking for me, so far from Tehran?"

"I'm not sure, Fatima, but we have to assume your husband and the Revolutionary Guards know you were the source of the leak. The story about Iranian involvement in the terrorist attacks is everywhere in the news. I hope you can forgive me for putting you in such a dangerous situation." Martin still blamed himself for failing to to prevent Fatima's abduction in Vienna.

"I'm sure you'll find a way to make it up to me," Fatima suggested, hoping to put Martin's mind at ease.

"Well, that's a welcome challenge." Martin smiled. "But I fear we have some ground to cover before we can rest. It's too dangerous here in Azerbaijan. If we drive all day, we can reach the Georgian border by nightfall. You'll be safe there."

As they drove north and then west toward the mountainous border between Azerbaijan and the Republic of Georgia, Martin and Fatima listened to the latest news reports on a shortwave radio. The BBC broadcast faded in and out but the message was clear enough; the entire region was in turmoil.

When the broadcast ended, Fatima fell sound asleep, curled up on her side in the backseat. Martin's mind continued to race as he tried to anticipate everything that could go wrong during their escape. After an hour or so, he was able to relax a bit and allowed himself to turn inward.

At some point in his career, Martin recognized the corrosive effects of his unusual profession. The constant need to project sincerity and empathy when dealing with prospective and recruited agents began to hollow out his reserves of humanity. That's why so many operations officers morphed into absolute bastards when their professional switches were turned off. Many simply lost the ability to behave in a civilized manner in their relations with one another. More than a few seemed to relish every opportunity to destroy their own kind. Many of them were hardened prostitutes, professional cynics who had lost the ability to feel anything beyond anger, contempt and ridicule. Such men sneered at any show of sincerity or weakness, as the wolf sneers before he devours the lamb.

Martin's experience was different, but still destructive. He felt more empathy for the weak as he grew older, but denied himself the right to hold aspirations for his own life. He would go out of his way to help a stranger, but seemed incapable of building a lasting relationship with a woman. He would risk his own life to keep the confidence of an agent, but found it impossible to trust his friends and acquaintances.

The emotions Martin had experienced as a young man stood out more sharply in his mind than anything he was capable of feeling in middle age--until now. As his spirit rebelled against the heart-numbing shackles of his profession, Martin allowed himself to ride high and free on waves of pure emotion, for the first time in many years.

He was afraid to lay down his internal armor, at first. Years of discipline and self-denial had worn deep tracks in his soul, and the wheels of his emotional baggage train were hard to pull out of the muck. It would have been impossible on his own, without Fatima, because she was the living memory of a younger, truer self, a man who was capable of giving and receiving love. As he drove west toward Georgia, Martin resolved to shatter the last remaining shards of ice encasing his heart, so he would know what it means to live.

At the same hour, an avaricious and recently-recruited Iranian intelligence officer met his Russian handlers at a safehouse in Moscow. The apartment was located in a convenient neighborhood, far enough from the Iranian embassy to avoid unwanted encounters with his colleagues, but close enough to allow the man to slip out for short meetings on a regular basis.

The Iranian gave his handlers a thumb drive with all of the secret cables he received from Tehran earlier that morning. Some of the documents described preparations for the expected American attacks. One report provided a detailed description of Fatima and accused her of leaking allegedly false information on the shipment of Russian nuclear weapons through Iran to Al-Qaeda, which accounted for the inflammatory reports everyone had seen in the media. The report also addressed concerns that Fatima was working as an Israeli or American spy and might attempt to flee the country.

Within hours, the report was briefed to Prime Minister Putin and the chiefs of Russia's security services.

Orders were issued to locate and detain Fatima immediately.

Early the next morning, every Russian intelligence
officer in the region relayed an urgent request for assistance. The officers were charged with contacting all of
the friendly intelligence and security services in Central
Asia to relay a false report that Fatima was a dangerous
Chechen terrorist traveling on an alias Iranian passport.
Russian intelligence still enjoyed considerable influence
in the republics of Armenia, Azerbaijan and Turkmenistan, so the requested assistance was provided with little
hesitation or reservation. In the Republic of Georgia, a
newly-independent state struggling to free itself from
Russian domination, the SVR had to rely on clandestine
penetrations of the Georgian government. That took a
little more time.

Chapter 35: The Survivor

Secretly, Ali Akbar Kalbasi's father was a life-long Communist, a bitter foe of European imperialism and a secret ally of the Soviet Union. Ali's father was a clever man and owed much to the special training he received from his KGB handlers during and after WWII. He was clever enough to divine the future, and with encouragement from his Russian handlers, he had developed a most fortuitous cover: Abu Ali, the "father of Ali" as he was known within the family, was an Iranian mullah.

The Soviet Union gained valuable experience dealing with the "Muslim problem" in the early 1930s. A fierce band of Muslim fighters, the Bashmanchi, was based in the Fergana Valley, an important center of Sunni religious fervor in Central Asia. The Bashmanchi earned the distinction of being the last surviving opponents of the Bolshevik Revolution, until they were finally defeated by the Red Army.

Although the Bashmanchi's hit-and-run tactics proved effective, and served as a lasting legacy for other Muslim insurgent groups, the group was finally defeated by an act of deception. In one of the most brilliant operations in its history, the KGB co-opted the Bashmanchi's leadership--just as they managed to co-opt the most important Russian anti-Communist groups in Europe and America in the 1920s--by secretly sponsoring and controlling ostensible anti-Soviet organizations all over the world.

A Soviet operative with extensive experience in the Fergana Valley later served as the KGB's senior officer in Tehran during the last years of WWII. A brilliant man, Oleg Petrovich Smirnov very nearly succeeded in bringing Iran under the Soviet Union's sphere of influence after the war, had it not been for meddling by the British and the Americans.

One of Smirnov's many gifts was his ability to recognize and cultivate talent. With the gift of foresight, Smirnov recruited Ali's father, Abu Ali--whose Communist sympathies were unknown outside Paris, where he had studied in the late 1930s--and steered him toward Iranian religious schools and the mosque. At the end of his long career, Colonel Smirnov served as an instructor at the KGB's training academy and mentored a promising young officer by the name of Boris Nikolayevich Mystikov, who expressed an abiding interest in Central Asia.

That's how Boris came to know one of Smirnov's most capable agents, the Iranian mullah and secret Communist Abu Ali; many years later, Boris was introduced to the son. Abu Ali was nothing if not thorough and had carefully prepared his son to follow in his footsteps. When the Shah finally fled Iran, Ali was well-positioned for a career as a Russian double agent.

Remarkably, Ali had been working for the Russians ever since, and had somehow managed to survive. As it turned out, survival was one of Ali's greatest gifts, a skill he would need over the next few days.

Ali wasn't particularly worried when his boss, Iranian Revolutionary Guards Colonel Sattar Fakoor, arrived unexpectedly in Zahedan, near the border with Pakistan, to supervise the execution of Bin Laden's favorite son. He was a little surprised when the Arab's wife and children were also slaughtered and their bodies burned, but sometimes that was the way things went in his business. And yes, Ali was a bit taken aback when it became clear the Colonel's boss, General Suleimani, didn't feel he could be trusted to take care of Awwab himself, but then the General didn't trust anyone.

No, the real shock came when Ali got an unexpected call from his Russian friend, just before Boris Nikolayevich made his last trip to Resurrection Island. Ali looked up to Boris, who had always treated him like a younger brother, so he was surprised when his experienced handler broke all the rules with an alarming telephone call several days before:

"My friend, we've been betrayed, we're all expendable. My life is forfeit and your life is in danger. You should flee the country immediately. Save yourself if you can."

And then the Russian hung up.

Ali had already seen the news reports in which the Russian government claimed it had rounded up and shot all of its citizens involved in the nuclear weapons deal, but he had assumed that was an elaborate cover story, mere propaganda. After the unexpected telephone call, however, Ali realized he might be expendable, too, if his Iranian bosses and the Russians wanted to erase any trace of their involvement in the affair.

A careful man, Ali was technically ready but emotionally unprepared to flee Iran. A closet homosexual his entire life (excellent training for a double agent, he thought), Ali would be forced to leave behind his favorite lover in Zahedan. No matter, he had another lover in Herat, in western Afghanistan, and he would serve as Ali's initial refuge.

Ali's lover, a handsome and well-educated Afghan working for the local NATO mission, was naive but reliable enough. He had just as much to lose as Ali if his homosexuality was exposed. Besides, the young Afghan believed Ali was simply a journalist, the cover story Ali used when traveling to Herat.

After a warm welcome and little sleep the night before, Ali asked his Afghan friend to make an introduction, a courtesy that was surprisingly easy to arrange. And that's how Ali found himself sitting in a seedy hotel room in Herat with a young British intelligence officer.

"First, Ali, let me tell you how pleased I am that you decided to contact us. This is a dangerous time for everyone and I'm confident you can help prevent further bloodshed."

"The only bloodshed I'm interested in preventing is my own. You and your American friends can bomb the mullahs to hell and back, as far as I'm concerned."

Ali's response was unexpected but the British intelligence officer, using the alias Peter, was well-trained and knew he should probe the Iranian's motivations.

"So help me understand, Ali, exactly why you've come to us." Peter leaned forward in his chair, in an attempt to match Ali's body language and level of intensity.

"It's simple," Ali responded. "If the Russians don't kill me, my own countrymen will. I want protection, for the rest of my life. I'm not talking about some Afghan refugee camp or a Pakistani ghetto in Birmingham. A nice flat in Bath would be better."

Ali had never been to England but he always enjoyed an active fantasy life. Living openly as a gay man in a secular society sounded like a dream come true. Ali was prepared to sell his soul for that, if the devil was willing to pay.

"By the way," Ali continued, "I intend to earn it."

"Well, Ali," Peter responded, "I believe you when you say you're a member of the Quds Force, based on what you've told me so far. I also believe you could be a very valuable friend, indeed. But you must understand, you're asking for the moon and the stars, so the decision will have to be made back in London, by some other celestial body."

Peter was encouraged when Ali laughed at his joke and settled back in his armchair with a more relaxed posture.

"Of course, of course," Ali responded, taking a sip of the chai provided by his host. "Here's what I'm willing to do, right here and right now," he continued. "I will provide you with enough information to prove that I have been working for the Russians all of my life, and my father before me. I'm confident our names will appear in your files. Secondly, I will provide enough information to prove that I know how Al-Qaeda managed to get its hands on the bombs."

"Oh, by the way," Ali added. "The Chechens had nothing to do with this, so that whole business with the attack on the Russian army base was a ruse, a very clever ruse."

Peter nodded his head quietly and got to work. He didn't have a great deal of experience, but he knew enough to realize this could be the real deal. The initial debriefing took a couple of hours, but when he was done, Peter was sure his colleagues would sell their souls to get their hands on Ali.

Less than 24 hours later, Ali was on a special flight to England in a Gulfstream executive jet with comfortable leather seats and an attractive male steward. "The British are perceptive, aren't they?" Ali wondered to himself.

Strictly speaking, Ali was a liar and a sociopath, but he was a clever man and knew how to exploit a good thing. He told the British almost everything he knew, saving just a little, for the sake of principle.

Chapter 36: A Land of Milk and Honey

Martin and Fatima spent the night in the ruins of an ancient monastery on the Georgian side of the border with Azerbaijan. The foundation of the monastery was laid in 460 AD, at a time when the Kingdom of Georgia was a small but respected ally of the Byzantine Empire. Tragically, the monastery was destroyed by Mongol invaders in the 13th century and never rebuilt.

Nowadays, the jagged pile of rock and stone served as a way station for armed smugglers, two of whom had been tasked with escorting the foreign couple on foot through a nearby mountain pass to avoid the usual border controls. The men were pleased to accept Martin's black Volga automobile as a "gift," to be re-documented and driven across the border from Azerbaijan in the future.

The two Georgian men sat on a pile of dark rocks near a small fire in the hollow of a ravine, preparing a meal with a fews bit of mutton and onion suspended on sharp sticks over the fire. They served the food on makeshift platters of Georgian flatbread, washed down with a flask of red wine.

Martin was thrilled to be back in the Republic of Georgia, despite the dangers he and Fatima faced until they could find refuge. As a younger man, Martin had spent two of the most productive years of his life in the small, mountainous country, shortly after the Georgian people gained independence from the Soviet Union. Martin's first assignment as a Chief of Station had been in the capital city of Tbilisi, and he had reveled in the chance to spread his wings, to exercise his judgment and to see the results of his work.

Over the years, he often wondered why he had such a natural affinity for the people of Georgia and their beautiful land. Perhaps it was because his Scots-Irish ancestors shared much in common. Martin was sure his Georgian friends would feel perfectly at home in the close-knit, clannish communities of southern Appalachia. Whatever the reason, Martin experienced a deep sense of connection with the people of Georgia and marveled at the country's natural beauty, which was only surpassed by the richness of its culture. The language, music and dance of the Georgian people were remarkable and on par with the Irish, another small nation that somehow managed to survive in the shadow of a more powerful, more aggressive neighbor. Surely there had to be some kind of connection: a bright cultural spark generated by a nation's will to resist oppression?

Martin didn't know the two men entrusted to guide them across the border, but he knew the head of their clan from his earlier assignment, and had dined with him years ago in his small village under a huge arbor surrounded by rich vineyards. The chieftain, Eduard Pardashvili, had never met an American who bothered to learn his native tongue, much less a foreigner who showed so much respect for his country's culture and traditions. To honor his new friend, Eduard had hosted a feast that had lasted until early the next morning, as only a Georgian could do. That experience, especially the music and unrestrained laughter, formed one of Martin's most cherished memories.

During a hike in the mountains surrounding the village, Martin forged a lasting alliance with Eduard. Martin had given Eduard the weapons he needed to protect his clan from the rampant lawlessness that plagued his young country; in return, Eduard had served as Martin's eyes and ears along Georgia's eastern and southern borders. No matter what he said in his messages back to Washington, Martin never thought of Eduard as a paid agent, but rather as his friend and ally.

That's why the two young men chosen to accompany Martin treated him with so much respect and deference. They didn't know who he was and they didn't ask. But they were determined to fulfill Eduard's strict orders and deliver the couple safely to their village in the morning.

After a sleepless night, with little more than a handful of blankets to comfort them, the group of three men and a woman arrived at Eduard's compound two hours after sunrise. Martin embraced his old friend warmly and they exchanged kisses in the Georgian style.

Eduard led the group directly to a long table under the same great arbor that had served as his family's outdoor banquet room for generations. On this morning, the table was covered with fresh Georgian flatbread, fruit, yoghurt, cheese, hot tea and sparkling mineral water from Tbilisi. Reenergized after their long walk by Eduard's warm greeting, Martin and Fatima seated themselves quickly and gratefully accepted his generous hospitality.

Unfortunately, Martin's enemies had their own eyes and ears on the Azerbaijani side of the border. The aggressive SVR Resident at the Russian embassy in Baku was hungry for promotion, and eager to attract the attention of Prime Minister Putin. He pushed every asset at his disposal until he stumbled across a report that an Azeri truck driver claimed to have seen the same woman the Iranians were looking for climbing into a black Volga sedan not far from the border crossing with Iran. With a little detective work, the Russians were able to link the Volga with Martin and his Irish passport. Two hours later the Resident, in coordination with his headquarters in Moscow, had positively identified Martin as a CIA officer who had served in the Republic of Georgia.

The Resident continued to push his men through the night until they reached a breakthrough: the Volga sedan Martin had purchased in Baku was located in an Azerbaijani border town. After local informants--smugglers who happened to be some of Eduard's bitterest rivals--identified two of Eduard's men as the new owners, a team of Russian Spetznaz, or Special Forces soldiers, found themselves concealed on a ridge overlooking Eduard's village.

The team was accustomed to making brief incursions across the Georgian border, which wasn't respected by the Russian government, so the soldiers had no trouble mounting an overwatch before dawn. The first reports were optimistic; it was clear the village was expecting guests. When three men and a woman were spotted as they emerged from a small mountain path, the call went out: targets identified.

Shortly after Martin and Fatima left the table to prepare for their onward journey to Tbilisi, two unmarked helicopters swept down on the valley and raked the village with rockets and machinegun fire. When the helicopters finished their second pass, the Speznaz team rained mortar fire down on the survivors.

Eduard tried to mount a defense in his sturdy farmhouse and the village's traditional stone tower, but his lightly-armed men were no match for the heavy weapons employed by the Russians. Still, his people had not managed to survive in such a dangerous neighborhood without maintaining some means of escape.

As Eduard huddled with his wife and sons in the cellar of the stone tower, he pulled Martin close and shouted in his ear: "You must lead the women and children to safety, do you understand?"

"Come with us, Eduard, show us the way!" Martin urged.

"No!" Eduard responded emphatically. "My oldest son and I will stay, to buy some time and to make the Russians pay for what they have done."

A rocket explosion shook the tower and dust fell from the beamed ceiling as Eduard stumbled toward a heavy wooden door, which he opened to reveal a narrow tunnel carved in the rocks by a forgotten generation of his ancestors. "There's no time to argue," Eduard shouted, "you must go!"

Martin embraced Eduard briefly as one of the Georgian's younger sons entered the tunnel with a lantern in hand. A small group of men, women and children entered the tunnel and moved quickly through a series of sharp turns before the tunnel straightened out into a noticeable downhill slope. After a considerable distance, the narrow passageway eventually opened up into a large natural cavern with a small opening on the opposite side just large enough for a grown man to crawl through.

As the group raced toward the cavern exit, the crack of a sharp explosion reverberated down the tunnel behind them, followed by a cloud of dust as the stone tower collapsed and buried its defenders, along with the entrance to the tunnel.

Martin and Fatima emerged from the cavern coughing and shielding their eyes as they adjusted to the sunlight, which seemed bright even at the bottom of a narrow ravine, a mere crevice on the far side of the mountain.

"Come quickly!" Eduard's son shouted, as he led the way down a barely perceptible path. "We won't be safe until we reach my uncle's village, a long march from here!"

Turning behind him, Martin hoisted a toddler on his shoulders as the child's mother, Eduard's second and much younger wife, followed with tears in her eyes. Time seemed to slow to a crawl as the group made its way down the trail to the village, a brief way station on the road to safety. The air was crisp and the fragrance of pines clung to the rocks on both sides of the ravine. Martin grieved for Eduard but savored every breath of this second life, the rebirth that followed every close call, every narrow escape. Not for the first or the last time, he wondered how many more lives he had to risk.

Martin and Fatima shared brief glances at every opportunity--full of emotion but empty of words--until they reached Tbilisi, home to helping hands.

When the Spetznaz team swept through Eduard's burning village, they shot all the survivors they could find and pulled the bodies from the rubble, arranging them in a bloody row in an open field. All the bodies were badly mangled but one corpse, missing its face but otherwise fitting Fatima's description, was loaded on a Russian helicopter and flown across the border to a small military base in Azerbaijan. Two days later, Russian experts identified the body as that of Eduard's sister. By then, Martin and Fatima had slipped away.

The day after the attack, Russia's state-controlled media described the incident as another example of the Republic of Georgia's inability to control armed criminal gangs operating inside its territory. The report was paired with a documentary on a recent Russian Army operation in South Ossetia, a breakaway province of Georgia, that ostensibly proved Georgia's culpability in allowing Chechen separatists to operate in the region, including terrorists involved in procuring the tactical nuclear weapons used in the recent attacks on Russia and America.

Some weeks later, Prime Minister Putin began planning the effective re-conquest of Georgia, using proxies to install a pro-Russian government. The campaign began with allegations that Georgia was preparing an invasion of Abkazia, a breakaway region on the Black Sea with close ties to Russia. Official expressions of concern by the American government were ignored.

Chapter 37: A Debt of Honor

More than a year had passed since Martin survived the Russian special forces attack on Eduard's village. The American remembered his friend as he sat in an isolated hut with several leaders of the Georgian resistance, deep in the shadow of the Caucasus mountains. During the previous summer, the Russian Army easily overwhelmed the Republic of Georgia's defense forces and quickly occupied Tbilisi, Batumi and several smaller cities. That came as no surprise, given the success of the initial Russian operation in the summer of 2008, which served as a useful dry run for a full invasion.

The Russian Army's ability to eliminate resistance in the countryside had not improved since the Soviet Union's defeat in Afghanistan, however, and the war was no longer going well for Prime Minister Putin. Not that the Russian people knew anything about that, as the remaining vestiges of a free press were eliminated well before the invasion. Always willing to learn, even from his opponents, Putin adopted a practice used by the Bush administration during the wars in Iraq and Afghanistan and forbade any media coverage on the steady flood of dead and wounded soldiers arriving at Russian train stations.

When Martin learned President Obama had signed a presidential directive authorizing a covert action campaign intended to provide both overt and covert support to Georgian freedom fighters, he decided not to retire after all and instead volunteered for duty on the front lines of a new cold war. He had more reason than most to join the fight, to repay Eduard for saving Fatima's life. It took some doing, but Martin eventually overcame earlier problems with his polygraph by confessing his sins and making Fatima available for a complete debriefing. The fact that Martin was one of only three officers in the entire Clandestine Service who spoke enough Georgian to do the job didn't hurt, either.

Martin and Fatima were only able to share a few months of peace together in America before his departure, but Fatima shared Martin's sense of obligation and understood why he had to go back. She was willing to wait for Martin in a small town outside Asheville, North Carolina, where she found work she loved in a private kindergarden. Although Fatima would never have a child of her own again, she found a sense of fulfillment caring for a Georgian child she and Martin adopted together, a four-year-old girl orphaned during the Russian invasion. With her heart lost in the desert for so many years, Fatima was surprised to discover she had so much love to give.

Not long after her arrival in Asheville, Fatima developed a close friendship with an American artist, an energetic widow who seemed to be the driving force behind many of the city's most active charities. Catherine Davis was a remarkable woman, in many ways, but her greatest gift was her ability to motivate others, to find talented women and introduce them to new passions that merited their time and attention.

Fatima first met Catherine at a charity auction in Asheville. When Martin wandered off to enjoy some music provided by a local jazz ensemble, Fatima stopped to admire a set of watercolors in a small booth. Most of the paintings featured playful children in local settings: little boys swimming in a mountain stream, two sisters riding an old horse in a summer field, a young family enjoying a picnic by a waterfall.

The paintings sketched a smile on Fatima's face as she circled the booth. She nodded politely at the artist, an older woman sitting quietly under a nearby redbud tree, and turned around to enjoy the last of the paintings. Fatima stopped suddenly and gazed with amazement at a beautiful depiction of Jamshideh Park, at the base of the Kolakchal Mountains, just outside Tehran. The painting perfectly captured the sense of magic she remembered as she strolled along the park's beautiful walkways with her father. Jamshideh was only a short drive from her childhood home in the Niavaran district of Tehran and had been one of her father's favorite spots for family outings.

Fatima barely noticed as the older woman approached her.

"Do you recognize the park?" Catherine asked.

Fatima turned around quickly and laughed when she saw a warm smile breaking across a wrinkled but healthy face.

"Yes, I do! It's outside Tehran. My father used to take me there when I was a child! But, how did you...?"

"I thought you might be Persian!" Catherine explained, as she introduced herself. "You look so familiar, like some of the women I knew when I lived in Tehran, before the Revolution."

"You must be kidding!" Fatima replied in wonder. "You're the first person I've met here who's ever been to Tehran. So few Americans visit these days."

"I know, it's sad," Catherine continued. "I wish I could go back myself, but they won't give me a visa.

230

My husband worked at the American Embassy, under the Shah, and the Iranian Government doesn't want me back."

"That's amazing!" Fatima said. "When did you live there?"

"In the early seventies, before the real troubles began. My husband was Counselor for Cultural Affairs and the art scene in Tehran was remarkable. He spent most of his time organizing exchanges for artists and musicians and I spent most of my time trying to improve my work."

"That's so strange!" Fatima exclaimed. "My mother was an artist, and we lived very close to the park you depicted in the painting. That's Jamshideh, isn't it?" she asked.

Thrilled to have met someone with a connection to her past, Catherine clasped Fatima's forearms and asked, "What was your mother's name?"

"She was also called Fatima. Her husband, my father, was Professor Aref Lavasani. Did you know them?"

"Yes, of course!" Catherine answered, with the same sense of wonder. "Fatima was an gifted artist. I loved her paintings of Tehran's old neighborhoods, the ones that were torn down by the Shah. We used to meet at the Farhangsara, in Niavaran. Wait a minute, we have to sit down, this is too much!"

Fatima followed Catherine over to a pair of folding chairs in the shade and sat down next to the older woman as they continued to hold each other's hands.

"Fatima," she continued, "did your mother ever bring you to the Art House? I remember meeting her there, once, and she had a beautiful daughter, a young girl, not yet 14."

"I don't know about the beautiful part," Fatima responded in the self-effacing Persian style, "but that must have been me! My mother always took me everywhere."

Fatima didn't remember Catherine from Tehran. As a girl, she was too distracted by all of the excitement at the art house to notice an older woman outside her mother's regular circle, but she was completely happy to have met someone who had known her mother, a warm-hearted American who understood Persia's rich history and shared so many of her interests.

Catherine was a very perceptive woman, and she recognized the need to help Fatima find an outlet for her energy, to help her make friends and integrate herself in the community. By the time Martin left for Georgia, Fatima was filling her days in meaningful ways, helping single mothers who were hit hard by the recession, when she wasn't working at the kindergarden. Fatima was also there to help Catherine set up her paintings at local venues, a task that had become more difficult as she grew older.

Fatima found peace in the mountains and would never leave. She missed Martin dearly, but was no longer completely dependent on him. She was mature enough to know that would make their reunion all the sweeter when he finally came home.

As Fatima settled into her new life in America, Martin was preparing a report on the situation in Georgia which he planned to relay to Headquarters later that evening. After months of bitter fighting, with weapons and ammunition provided by the CIA, Georgian freedom fighters had begun to put the Russians on the defensive. The situation on the ground fit a familiar pattern; using the same brutal tactics they'd employed in Chechnya, the Russians were able to hold major Georgian cities, though they were unable to hold the countryside.

The Russians held a clear advantage on the Black Sea coast, where they could resupply their forces with direct support from the Russian Navy, but they faced a distinct disadvantage in the interior, where their supply lines stretched through dangerous mountain passes. The situation was further complicated when a team of Georgian commandos, using munitions provided by the Americans, destroyed the huge tunnel the Russians used to move supplies and reinforcements into Georgian territory.

And so it was that Martin answered his lifelong calling and picked up where he left off during the Soviet invasion of Afghanistan all those years ago. Older and more experienced, the veteran spy was determined to do everything he could to make the Russians pay for the attack on Eduard's village and the invasion of his adopted daughter's homeland. Martin only hoped his own government would do a better job learning from the past.

When he first supported the Afghans in their struggle against the Red Army, Martin was young and had much to learn about human nature. At the time, he was amazed by the stupidity of the Soviets, who dared to occupy a proud and ancient land with a reputation for humiliating foreign invaders, and had assumed America was incapable of making the same mistake.

Years later, his eyes were opened when the United States invaded Iraq. He was struck by the symmetry, the inevitability of both errors. It was a remarkable man who could avoid overreaching when he achieved the height of his powers. It happened every day on a human scale, with aging athletes who couldn't stop playing, even when they were losing; with popular politicians who couldn't resist temptation, even when they were winning; with successful businessmen who could never earn enough money, as their egos always seemed to grow faster than their bank accounts.

The pattern was most obvious in a long list of conquerors-- the Alexanders, Napoleons, and Hitlers of the world--but was just as evident in lesser tyrants; petty, vindictive men who were driven to dominate others in all walks of life.

Martin also understood why his own country's fall from the pinnacle of power was inevitable: when things appeared to be going well, people resisted change. Only pain brings change; not the possibility, but the reality, especially for generations of Americans who had never known hardship.

Sure, Martin thought, it would have been great if he could have weaned himself from his personal addiction to oil, before the painful consequences of inaction forced him do so. It would have been nice if his family and friends could have set aside more of the riches they accumulated during the bubble years, rather than wasting away in an orgy of consumption. It would have been wonderful if America had nurtured the spirit of cooperation exhibited by the rest of the world after 9/11, rather than starting an unnecessary war in Iraq. And what if the U.S. had stopped coddling Arab dictators, just to keep the cheap oil flowing, many years before those dictators engendered a wave of Islamic extremism directed at the West?

But that wasn't the way the world worked, given the vagaries of human nature. Sometimes, even the smartest people had to fall down hard, flat on their faces, before they could see the truth. Sometimes, even Americans were at their best when faced with adversity, even when climbing out of a pit they dug for themselves. The misguided Global War on Terrorism, and the economic bubble that finally burst in 2008, were two such pits, and they probably wouldn't be the last.

Martin clung to the hope that his countrymen would continue to learn the value of prudence and humility. He hoped they would be mature and confident enough to build on the tough lessons learned and the deep wisdom gained, as other Americans had done in the past. He knew every generation had to rely on its own experience, and he was sure future generations would make their own mistakes. He simply hoped his generation, and the young people who followed them, would be strong enough to see the country through the latest crisis.

Glossary

Al-Qaeda: The terrorist organization founded by Usama Bin Laden during the struggle against Soviet forces in Afghanistan. The Arabic word "Al-Qaeda" means "the base."

Baluchistan: A province of Pakistan with a distinct ethnic and cultural identity and a long border with Iran.

Caliphate: A term used to describe righteous governments early in the history of Islam that modern Muslims regard as the golden age of Islamic civilization. Baghdad served as the capitol of an important Caliphate. As a result, the U.S. invasion and occupation of Iraq holds special significance for many Muslims.

Chechnya: A tiny, mountainous region of the Russian Federation that has struggled unsuccessfully for independence from Moscow for centuries. Islam is the dominant religion in Chechnya and some Chechens have aligned themselves with Usama Bin Laden.

Clandestine Service: The operational arm of the Central Intelligence Agency (CIA) tasked with collecting foreign intelligence and conducting covert action.

GRU: Russian military intelligence.

FSB: The Russian Federal Security Service, a successor to the Soviet KGB with responsibility for domestic security.

IRGC: Iran's Revolutionary Guards Corps, which serves as the main defender of the Islamic revolution in Iran.

KGB: The Soviet Committee for State Security, which was divided into foreign (SVRR) and domestic (FSB) components after the collapse of the USSR.

Mossad: Israel's foreign intelligence service.

Polygraph: A term used to describe both the equipment needed to conduct a lie detector test and the test itself.

Spetznaz: Russian special forces commandos.

Quds Force: The elite paramilitary arm of the IRGC, which provides support to terrorist organizations like Hezbollah.

Shia: A minority of Muslims worldwide belong to the Shia sect, the members of which were often persecuted by the majority Sunni sect after their leader, the Prophet Muhammad's grandson, Husayn, and his supporters were defeated at the Battle of Karbala. A majority of Iranian and Iraq Muslims are Shia.

Shin Bet: Israel's domestic security service.

Sunni: A majority of Muslims worldwide belong to the the Sunni sect, which gained dominance after its adherents defeated the prophet Muhammad's grandson, Husayn, at the Battle of Karbala.

SVRR: The Russian Foreign Intelligence Service, a successor to the Soviet KGB.

WMD: Weapons of mass destruction, a term often used to describe chemical, biological and nuclear weapons.

Zulfiqar: The legendary two-pointed sword of The Prophet Muhammad, who gave the weapon to his cousin and most faithful companion, Ali, to recognize his courage in battle. Ali's son Husayn bin Ali, who was also the Prophet's grandson, later carried the sword when he was martyred at the Battle of Karbala in the area now known as Iraq. This ancient battle lead to a schism between Sunni and Shia Islam which continues to this day.

Cast of Characters

Ahmed: A young Pakistani from the province of Baluchistan who tried to volunteer information on suspected terrorists to an American official working at the U.S. consulate in Karachi.

Thomas Hart Benton III: The U.S. Ambassador in Beirut, Lebanon who was involved in negotiations with the government of Iran.

Awwab Bin Laden: The son of Usama Bin Laden who facilitated Al-Qaeda's secret relationship with the Iranian Revolutionary Guards Corps (IRGC)'s paramilitary arm, the Quds Force.

Philippe Broussard: A member of Al-Qaeda; the son of a French Canadian mother and an Algerian immigrant father.

Steve Campbell: A senior watch officer at the National Counterterrorism Center in Northern Virginia.

Convoy: The code name for an Iranian citizen and ethnic Kurd who owned a trucking company and worked as an American spy.

Fernando Cruz: An alias identity used by Filipino Muslim terrorist Abu Assam, a member of Al-Qaeda working under cover on a merchant ship with frequent port calls in the United States.

Catherine Davis: An artist and community activist in Asheville, North Carolina who lived in Iran under the Shah, when her husband was assigned to the U.S. Embassy in Tehran.

Brian Kelly: An overworked security officer at the U.S. consulate in Karachi whose interview with the Pakistani volunteer Ahmed was interrupted by a terrorist attack.

Colonel Sattar Fakoor: A senior officer of the Iranian Revolutionary Guards Corps (IRGC)'s paramilitary arm, the Quds Force. Colonel Fakoor was also the husband of Fatima Lavasani.

Dr. Samantha Jones: A professor at the University of Wisconsin and author of the book "Terrorism and Democracy."

Ali Akbar Kalbasi: A member of the Iranian Revolutionary Guards Corps (IRGC)'s paramilitary arm, the Quds Force. Kalbasi leads two secret lives: As a gay man trying to survive in the Islamic Republic of Iran, and a Russian spy.

Mariam Khoury: A successful Lebanese-American businesswoman from New Orleans serving part-time as an Israeli spy.

Ephraim Kodar: A senior Israeli intelligence officer working for the Mossad in Vienna, Austria.

Fatima Lavasani: An educated Persian woman, the daughter of an Iranian professor who taught in the United States and the wife of Colonel Sattar Fakoor, a senior officer in the Iranian Revolutionary Guard (IRGC).

John Martin McCrary: A senior operations officer in the CIA's Clandestine Service. Martin's father, William aka "Billy" McCrary, was a gambler and convicted felon from South Carolina. His mother, the Lebanese woman Maria Sedari, worked as an entertainer at mafia-owned casinos in Las Vegas and Havana.

Javad Mostaghim: The Iranian Ambassador in Beirut, Lebanon who was involved in negotiations with the United States.

Boris Nikolayevich Mystikov: A Russian intelligence officer from the Foreign Security Service (FSB), a successor to the Soviet Committee for State Security (KGB).

Eduard Pardashvili: A local leader in the Republic of Georgia who maintained a secret relationship with the CIA.

Father Paul: A Jesuit Priest and Professor of Philosophy at Loyola University in New Orleans who recognized Martin McCrary's talent when he was a student at Tulane University and introduced him to recruiters from the Central Intelligence Agency (CIA).

Jacques Pitard: An Al-Qaeda operative; the son of a French father and an Algerian mother.

David Polansky: A linguist working for the National Security Agency (NSA). His wife Amy works as a nurse at the Walter Reed Army Medical Center, treating wounded soldiers returning from the wars in Iraq and Afghanistan.

Janet Reid: Deputy Chief of Mission at the U.S. Embassy in Beirut, Lebanon.

Oleg Petrovich Smirnov: A legendary KGB expert on Central Asia who recruited Ali Akbar Kalbasi's father after World War II.

Todd Smith: A CIA officer and Chief of Station at the U.S. Embassy in Beirut, Lebanon.

Brigadier General Suleimani: Commander of the Iranian Revolutionary Guards Corps (IRGC)'s paramilitary arm, the Quds Force.

Lieutenant Pavel Tarasov: A Junior officer in Russian military intelligence (GRU) who discovers he can make money selling secrets to Russian mafia figures.

Colonel Mark Tolliver: The Defense Attache at the U.S. Embassy in Beirut, Lebanon.

Viktor Viktorovitch Yadnikov: A former Soviet military scientist and expert on chemical and biological weapons.